FALLEN WISHES

THREE WISHES HISTORICAL FANTASY BOOK 3

MARCY KENNEDY

ALSO BY MARCY KENNEDY

CHAPTER 1

*N*othing with the fae was ever free.

Ceana Campbell rubbed at the throbbing pulse between her eyes. The cave around her had gone silent but for the steady rhythm of water dripping somewhere nearby from the ceiling to the rocky floor below.

The words Eliezer had spoken to her, Gavran, and Salome still hung in the air.

They want you to give them the name of the fairy who cursed you. Give them that, and they'll lift the curse. Give them that, and you'll be free to live out your lives like everyone else.

Heat flooded over her body. This once it would have been nice had the fae done something because it was the right thing to do. But, of course, they wouldn't. Of course, they'd rather barter for whatever benefit they could squeeze from the situation.

"I don't have the fairy's name." Her words came out angrier than she'd intended. But, truthfully, had the seelie court actually believed this was a reasonable request? "It's not like she introduced herself before setting the cursed wishes on us. Nor will she give us her name if we could find her and ask. Which we can't."

The heat drained as fast as it'd come and left a chill in its wake. They'd asked an impossible task. One guaranteed to fail. Perhaps they'd even done it on purpose to ensure she failed. If she failed, then no responsibility had to be taken. No wrong admitted. She'd be a scapegoat, led out into the desert to die for another's sins.

Gavran shifted closer to her and linked his fingers with hers, his palm pressed tight against hers. A communication without words that—whatever this meant for the future—she didn't have to face this alone.

Pressure built behind her eyes. The concept still seemed as foreign as trying to speak a language from a far-off country. Having allies—friends. She and Gavran weren't without resources, not the way they'd been when all of this first began. And they had each other again.

Gavran squeezed her hand gently and angled to face Eliezer. "Surely the seelie court will see reason if you explain it to them."

Eliezer shook his head. His spiky hair cast elongated, finger-like shadows on the walls in the lantern light. "I tried to change their minds. They will not. Their decision is final."

"How hard did you try?" Gavran's voice sounded more than a little skeptical. "Because other than Lady MacDonald, every fae we've had the misfortune of coming across has tried to trick or hurt us. Trust's a mite hard to come by."

"Eliezer's purpose among the fae is to be a helper." Salome's words were spoken softly from the far side of the cave, but the way the sound bounced from the ceiling and back down made it seem like she was standing beside them. "I can assure you his inability to help you is felt by him as if he were the one suffering the consequences."

The ache in Ceana's throat turned into a burn and trailed down into her belly. Eliezer's face was pinched, his lips tight as if he were fighting physical pain. The fae seemed not to care about hurting their own, either. "The seelie court is supposed to be good and fair. But they're punishing us for things we had nothing to do with."

Gavran's frown deepened. "I don't understand any of this. Why is the seelie court demanding proof before they'll lift the wishes from us? Someone needs to explain it." His lips twisted. "Slowly. As if I were a bairn newly learning to walk and talk."

Ceana held back a snort. For the past two weeks, he'd been the opposite of an innocent child, thanks to the poisoned wound the nuckalevee gave him in their battle. She'd praise the Almighty every day that the Gavran who wanted to kill her was finally gone and the Gavran who'd always protected her had returned to her.

But with how clouded his mind had been, it was no great surprise he didn't clearly remember everything that had been said or done around him.

Eliezer shifted his giant bulk on the boulder he'd chosen for a seat. He pursed his unnaturally thick lips, as if he were going to refuse the request.

Salome moved to his side, still graceful despite her ever-growing belly. She placed a hand on one of his fingers, making their difference in size impossible to ignore. She might as well have wrapped her hand around a branch. "Speaking plainly can't possibly cause more harm, old friend. The seelie court already assumes they know about our world, so you're not breaking any vows by revealing fae secrets to humans."

Ceana shifted her weight forward and parted her lips to tell him there couldn't be more than half a dozen people the whole world over who'd seen as much of the fae as they had at this point. Gavran squeezed her hand again and shook his head. She huffed but closed her mouth. Galling as it was, he was probably right. Eliezer needed Salome's peaceful influence to calm his fears, not her own tendency to charge in like an angry bull.

Eliezer blew out a long breath. The damp, earthy scent of moss wafted around the cavern. "I suppose that's true." He smiled, revealing teeth that looked strong enough to crush rocks. "And if they banish me, too, you've clearly no problem taking in strays." He pointed a beefy finger at Ceana and Gavran, and then pointed toward two smaller rocks nearby. "Sit. You're making me nervous with your hovering."

Salome eased herself down onto a ledge protruding from the wall on Eliezer's other side as if to set the example. Gavran followed suit, and Ceana let him pull her along with him. It'd only be petty to argue with him that she'd rather stand. The rock he picked for them was large enough to seat them both and smooth on the top, as if a massive force has cracked it cleanly away from the wall at some point in the past.

Eliezer's bushy eyebrows drew down, completely shadowing his eyes in the faint lantern light. "The war between the seelie and unseelie courts has been ongoing since before the fall of mankind into sin, that much you know from Scripture. Now the unseelie want the Almighty to forbid any fae, seelie or unseelie, from taking physical form without his permission. They claim the seelie court has become drunk on power and are abusing the privilege."

Gavran nodded his head. "That seems like it would be a good thing, then."

A tight, fluttering feeling rooted in Ceana's chest, and she ran a fingernail down a hairline crack in her rock seat. It should be a good thing. They'd witnessed firsthand the pain, grief, and suffering caused by unseelie fae like the nuckalevee, the banshee, and the baobhan sith roaming the world. The world would be better off if they couldn't take physical form anymore.

But the idea couldn't quite settle in her mind. It was like trying to walk in someone else's shoes. It rubbed and chaffed and fit poorly anyway she tried to move it. "The unseelie would never suggest something that would benefit humans."

Eliezer tilted his head to one side. "True. They would not. But they haven't succeeded in winning the war by being able to take physical form. People still believe in the Almighty One. As long as people believe in the supernatural world, it's not hard to also believe that an all-powerful creator exists."

The pieces slotted into place in her mind. "But if the fae aren't allowed to regularly take physical form anymore, then people will eventually stop believing in the supernatural."

Eliezer nodded.

"Aye, but how does that justify denying our request?" Gavran rubbed two fingers into his temple. His voice had the tone of someone whose head was beginning to ache and who merely wanted to go home. "Their squabbles have nothing to do with us. You both told us the cursed wishes should have never been allowed to go on this long in the first place. We should have been cured without having to ask."

"If an unseelie cursed you," Salome said matter-of-factly. "But that's not the case."

Gavran stiffened, and his gaze snapped to Ceana. Creases formed between his eyes. "You're not surprised. You knew this already?"

So much had happened in the fortnight the nuckalevee venom coursed through his veins. She tried to run it back in her mind. Had Gavran even been there when they'd discussed the nature of the fairy who'd cursed them? She couldn't recall, but she had the vague notion that it'd been during the short period of time when they'd been separated. And they'd had so much else happening since. "I knew."

His Adam's apple moved slowly up, then down. An expression she couldn't name flickered across his face. He opened his mouth, closed it. His chin came up. "But you didn't keep it from me intentionally? You thought I knew?"

The air sucked from her lungs. He still didn't trust her. And why should he. She'd known him for years. As far as he was aware, he'd known her little more than a month. All he had to go on beyond that was what she'd told him and the echoes he still felt. And look at all the times she'd withheld things, made decisions without him that should have been made together, and brought trouble down upon him.

His gaze stayed steady on her face, his expression vulnerable rather than angry. Questioning. She drew in a breath until her lungs seemed to press into her ribs. He hadn't made accusations. Instead of jumping to a conclusion and running with it, he'd chosen to stop and ask her. Maybe this was what it should be like between two people who loved each other. His desire for clarity wasn't an attack. Only her own guilt made it feel that way.

She met his gaze and held it. "I thought you knew. The only way the cursed wishes the fairy gave us could have allowed us to defeat the nuckalevee is if the fairy is seelie."

Gavran's shoulders came down. He brushed a piece of hair back from her face. "There always seems to be something important I've forgotten. Keep reminding me?"

Her throat tightened, and she nodded. They'd keep reminding each other of the important things.

Gavran let out a sigh and shifted his attention back to Eliezer. "So if what happened was an act of a seelie, then the unseelie court can say *here's proof for our case that no fae should be allowed physical form.* That's why the seelie court has abandoned us. They're demanding the fairy's name as proof we're not lying to help the unseelie."

Hearing Gavran speak the words drove the truth like a spear into Ceana's belly. She pressed a fist to the pain. They'd been given an impossible task. The seelie court had branded them liars, or at least told themselves they were in order to ease their own consciences over what they were doing to them. "This isn't right."

She looked up at Eliezer. The tips of his hair drooped, and he made no answer. He averted his gaze and rubbed his forefinger across his bulbous nose in a gesture that was eerily human and reeked of shame. At least that was something. He wasn't trying to defend what the seelie court was doing to them.

So many times, people had thought poorly of her. She'd thought poorly of herself. Often it'd even been warranted. But not this time.

She rose to her feet, her fists balled at her sides. "Why would they think we were working with the unseelie and willing to lie for them? With all the evil the unseelie have caused, why would any sane person help them?"

Eliezer shifted, and the rock creaked as if it might crumble underneath his weight. "Humans don't want to curb their desires. They want to be able to do whatever they want. They don't care whether it's right or wrong so long as it pleases them. The unseelie promise them whatever they want. There are many in this world who serve them instead of the Almighty."

Ceana shivered. That much she'd seen firsthand. "So what do we do? I don't have the fairy's name. I can't give the seelie court what they want. Is there nothing else we could offer them?" She turned to face Salome. "I could describe her the way I did for you."

Salome gave a tiny smile, but it quivered at the edges. "That convinced me because you described a fae more accurately than you should have been able to had you never seen one. Your description could fit many fae, however."

Gavran got to his feet as well and paced the floor. "Is there no other way to prove our innocence?"

Even Salome looked to Eliezer, making it clear without words that she didn't know of another way.

Eliezer shook his head.

Ceana forced her gaze to stay on Eliezer. She wouldn't look at Gavran as he stalked back and forth. He'd begged her to marry as soon as they returned to Duntulm Castle. He'd wanted them to become man and wife. She'd insisted they wait until after the curses were lifted. Where did that leave them now?

They could never have the life together that they wanted. The cursed wishes would always hang over her like a lethal illness, a single slip in focus, a single accidental separation all it took to destroy everything they built.

And her brother. Colin could be living in some dark alley, forced the eat the cast offs even the pigs wouldn't touch and vulnerable to anyone with ill motives who came along. She had no hope of finding and caring for him if she stayed under the curses.

She lifted her gaze to the ceiling of the cavern, as if somehow her prayers might reach the Almighty better that way. Stalactites hung overhead, but no answers. The Almighty wasn't going to audibly give her the fairy's name just because she asked. How often had Gavran's mamaidh told her that wasn't the way prayer worked? More often, the Almighty worked in and through his servants on earth.

The muscles in her back pulled so tight they threatened to snap. They'd come too far to give up now. They stood to lose too much. Their future. "The banshee seemed to know who we were. She'd heard of us before we met her. Someone must know the identity of the fairy who cursed us. Who can we ask?"

Eliezer cleared his throat with a sound like rocks grinding together. "The fuath might know. *Might*."

His voice was heavy, not the light, excited tone most people had when solving a problem.

She swallowed, the sound loud in her own ears. The fuath weren't one of the creatures her mamaidh told her stories about. She should ask questions. But the words wouldn't come. If she didn't ask, there was still a chance they'd be seelie. There was still a chance they wouldn't be another creature who wanted them dead far more than they wanted to help them do anything.

She glanced at Gavran. A muscle pulsed in his jaw as if he were clenching and unclenching his teeth.

His gaze shifted in her direction and stayed on her face. Almost as if he were asking permission to do what she couldn't. She nodded. Sooner started, sooner done—whatever that might mean.

Gavran sucked in a breath and turned back to Eliezer. "Are the fuath unseelie?"

CHAPTER 2

*E*liezer's lips turned down. "They are unseelie."

Ceana faced the cavern wall. She needed a moment —just one moment—to think. They were back to the same situation they'd had when they needed a cure for Gavran's supernatural poisoning. Those who might know were those least likely to tell them.

She pressed her palms against the stone. The air around them was unnaturally humid, the walls cool and damp to the touch. Almost like the place where they stood was a small bubble out of time and these were its boundaries.

If only it were and they could take all the time they needed to solve this problem before returning to the outside world. But time wouldn't stop for them. The tiny spider that drooped down in front of her assured her of that. It scurried back up its impossibly thin thread of web and disappeared into a hole. The world continued to go on. They had decisions to make. Turning her back on them wouldn't make them go away any more than hiding her face under the covers had solved her problems as a child.

She shifted to face Eliezer and Salome. Gavran had dropped

back onto the rock where they'd sat together moments before. He'd lowered his head into his hands and gripped clumps of his hair with his fists.

She moved to his side and placed a hand on his shoulder. He took one of his own out of his hair and laid it over hers, though he didn't look up. He'd gone with her through everything, but how much could he take before regrets and doubt poked their way in?

She glared at Eliezer. "And why will the fuath know when you don't? Why should we believe they'll have the answers?"

Salome's lips tightened in a look that would one day surely make her child stop whatever mischief he or she had gotten into.

Maybe her tone hadn't been as respectful toward Eliezer as a messenger from the Almighty and the seelie court deserved, but could anyone truly blame her? After all they'd recently gone through? To face yet another unseelie? It hardly seemed possible that they'd have to do it again, let alone that they could survive another encounter.

"The fuath are known for interbreeding with humans." Salome massaged her lower back. "But they can't do it by force. They have to use seduction, manipulation. So they study as many human-fae interactions as possible to learn more about human behavior. They're not all-knowing. It's possible they didn't observe what the fairy did to you. However, they are your best chance."

"I thought that was a myth, something lords made up to sound grander." Gavran raised his head and slowly straightened the rest of his body to follow. "There are actually people in the world with fae blood?"

One side of Salome's lips curved up. "Some. Not all who claim it truly have it, and it's impossible to prove."

"No supernatural powers, then?" Gavran's voice had the tone of someone who was making conversation to buy time. No doubt he didn't want to address the bigger issue yet either. "Horns? Longer lives?"

Salome gave him a full smile this time. "No supernatural powers. At most they're more sensitive to the supernatural realm than those without fae blood."

Eliezer made a harrumphing noise. "You've become more human than I realized, Salome. All this pointless chatter. None of that matters. We need to discuss the matter at hand. I can't stay here forever." His voice tightened. "I was only supposed to deliver the court's verdict."

Ceana sneaked a glance at him. His features were dissimilar enough from a human's that she couldn't quite read his expression. But he almost seemed nervous. She glanced at Salome. The mirth had left her face.

Salome smoothed a hand down the front of her already smooth skirt. "They'll call you to account for your time spent with us?"

Eliezer shifted. His large feet scuffed tracked in the dusty cavern floor. "If they think I've done more than I was tasked to do, I might be removed from this post. Whoever replaces me won't have compassion for any... infractions."

Gavran rose to his feet. "We apologize. We appreciate the risk you're taking for us. What do we need to know to face the fuath?"

Ceana's heart pushed against its constraints inside her chest. How did he pull himself together like that as soon as it was needed? Once again, he'd set aside his feelings in order to care for another. For multiple others. Eliezer losing his position would harm Salome and Lord MacDonald as well.

If they hadn't been around Salome and Eliezer, she would have kissed Gavran. Whatever such a good man saw in her, she might never know, but she could believe he saw it and work toward becoming that Ceana. The best version of her.

Eliezer stretched out his hands and cracked his knuckles. "Full-grown fuath won't give you information for free, and they won't trade for anything you're willing to give. They only accept one kind of payment."

Ceana's cheeks burned as if she'd leaned too close over a fire. Eliezer didn't have to say what that payment was for her to understand. Not when fuath were known for interbreeding with humans. And Eliezer was right. "I've no desire to become one more tally in a fuath ledger. So how do we get the information from them if they only want a payment we won't provide?"

"You'll have to approach an immature fuath." Salome exchanged a glance with Eliezer, almost as if she were checking her information with him before continuing. "They're known as brollachan."

The desire to draw back coursed over Ceana's body. The same strange revulsion had come over her the one time she'd seen a snake shifting out of its skin. Salome had admitted that the fae occasionally bred with humans, but somehow that hadn't seemed as bad as them reproducing on their own. Filling the world with more and more evil all the time.

"Are the stories wrong then?" Her voice came out reedier than she would have liked. Fear tugged at her edges. She imagined building up walls to keep it out. "My mamaidh always said they came into human beds because they couldn't have children any other way."

"*Immature* was the wrong choice of words." Salome pushed her lips together. "The fae world isn't as clear to me now as it once was. The longer I'm human, the more difficult it is for me to hold the details. Carrying my child seems to have escalated the process." She turned to Eliezer again.

His bushy eyebrows came together, nearly touching. "I think you mean *formless*. The Almighty has placed limits on the fae. The fuath can only take partners who are willing. A fuath who forces themselves on a human being breaks apart. Even that's not a perfect description, but there's no exact word for it in the human languages. They roam the world as a specter from that point on. A brollachan is one of the fuath who forced themselves upon a human and now can't bring their essence together to form a physical body anymore."

Bile burned at the back of her throat. The brollachan weren't young, naïve fuath who might be easily tricked. They were the vilest of their kind. Worse than the unseelie fae they'd faced in the past.

All the air in the cavern suddenly seemed used up. The smoke from the lanterns clogged her nose, burned her throat. She couldn't do it. It wasn't reasonable to ask anyone to keep facing monster after monster.

Gavran's strong arms slid around her. She turned in his hold and buried her face into him. Tucked in as tight as she could. The freshly laundered shirt the MacDonalds had given him still smelled faintly of the sharp bite of lye.

His heart beat steadily beneath her ear. She focused on the sound. So long as he kept his arms around her like this, she'd hold together. All the little pieces threatening to break off of her and leave her too broken to mend would hold together.

"Maybe it won't be so bad." Gavran's warm breath brushed against her hair. "Maybe it will be straightforward this time."

"You always were the one who believed apples would drop straight into his basket and sheep would lay still to be sheered just because he asked. Even before the wishes."

"One of us has to believe for the best."

Aye. The world would be a depressing place if it was filled only with people like her who missed the beams of sunlight because they were focused on all the surrounding shadows.

She pulled herself apart from Gavran. Eliezer had warned them only a few minutes ago that his time was limited. She could crumble later. For now, she had to be like Gavran. "What else can you tell us about the brollachan?"

Salome gave a tiny shake of her head and shrug.

Ceana turned to face Eliezer.

His jaw shifted as if he were clenching his teeth together. "The fuath and brollachan are the corrupted fae who once nurtured love and family. Now they break them." The anger in his voice was palpable.

Ceana ticked off the creatures they'd already fought in her mind. The nuckalevee, who fed on pain and suffering. The banshee, who fed on grief. The baobhan sith, who fed on the last of a person's life by convincing them to leave the earth before their time.

The reverse of each must have been what they were before they rebelled. The fuath and brollachan now wanted to break families apart. That information would help. She had no family left to break, and Gavran was already estranged from his. Gavran was the closest thing she had to family and the one she loved most, but she certainly wouldn't sacrifice their relationship in exchange for information.

She rubbed a hand across her forehead. They weren't going deep enough. The fuath and brollachan created families who weren't whole. But they did it by manipulation and seduction. If love and family were about sacrificing for the wellbeing of others, then perhaps what the brollachan thrived on was control. Forcing themselves on an unwilling partner would certainly fit that. They'd wanted it so badly that they'd been willing to risk their physical form to get it.

Ceana held back a shiver. The picture of the brollachan grew worse with every new piece of knowledge.

"What will a brollachan want in exchange for information?" Gavran asked.

The red of Eliezer's spiky hair deepened to the color of spilled wine and nearly blended in with the black streaks. His form merged with the shadows of the cave, then solidified again. "They are not like the banshee. It will depend on the mood of the individual brollachan. But if they know who you are, they will not want to help you. They will likely ask you to do something that violates what you believe to be right. They will want to both punish you and see how far they can make you go."

An unnatural combination of a shudder and a twang of elation went through Ceana. The brollachan was truly as awful as she'd thought, but she'd been right about their nature. And the better she understood the unseelie, the more likely she was to be able to survive.

Gavran slid his hand into hers and held tight. She clung back. Whether he'd done it for her comfort or for his didn't matter. Maybe that was how relationships were supposed to work anyway. You did something for the other, and you benefitted from it as well.

Gavran absently rubbed his thumb along the back of her hand. "What kinds of things might it ask us to do? Could it ask us to help it become a physical being again? From what you've said, that's one of the worst things I can imagine."

"They can't go back to physical form ever once they've been made into a wraith. You can be certain it won't be that."

A fragment of what Eliezer had originally said poked at Ceana's mind and wouldn't give way. "What does it matter if it knows who we are? Won't it treat us the same either way?"

Eliezer drew in air, but it didn't come out again. As if he'd forgotten that in human form breathing went both ways. "The brollachan now see other unseelie as their family. They're the only unseelie fae who care what happens to other unseelie."

Gavran stiffened beside her. "And we killed the nuckalevee."

Eliezer dipped his head. Then his gaze shifted above them, as if listening to a voice they couldn't hear. He rose to his feet. "I have to return."

What? Nay. Ceana stepped toward him, her hands outstretched. "Wait. We don't know enough yet."

Eliezer's form wavered. The lantern flames sucked towards

him slightly. "I'm sorry. I would stay longer if I could. Find one who's possessed, and you'll find a brollachan."

Then he was gone.

CHAPTER 3

"*W*ill we never be free of horses?" Gavran cast a teasing look in Ceana's direction.

Ceana forced a smile to her lips for his sake. He was clearly trying to lighten the heavy mood that had fallen on her since Eliezer's parting words. She had said more than once that this was the last time he'd have to ride a horse. And yet he kept being forced back onto one. In this case, for their return trip from Eliezer's cavern to Duntulm Castle.

Lord MacDonald lifted Salome onto the back of her own mount, his hands lingering a little longer than necessary on his wife's sides. They'd apparently been inside longer than Ceana had realized. When she, Gavran, and Salome emerged, Lord MacDonald, Eachann, and Lyall were arguing about whether Lord MacDonald should go inside to search. Or, more accurately, Lord MacDonald and Eachann were arguing, and Lyall had been trying to mediate between them.

"Your fae contact wants them to exorcize a demon?" Lord MacDonald asked. "That sounds like work for a priest to me. Or at least needing lessons from a priest."

"Not exorcize a demon." Salome gathered up her reins. "Merely speak to a person who's been possessed."

Merely? Ceana held back a snort. When had contact with the unseelie fae been *merely* anything. She should have guessed where this would lead once she recognised brollachan thrived on control. The brollachan no longer had a body of its own, and there could be no greater form of control than inhabiting that of another and forcing them to do your bidding.

Eachann threw himself onto the back of his horse. "This is all madness if you ask me. Not that any of you ever seem to ask."

"Don't feel bad, lad." Lyall pushed his wire-rimmed glasses higher on his nose. "That's the way of it for me as well. I'm beginning to think it's for the best. What I know is already enough. If they asked my opinion on anything not medical, I'd have to hear even more." His tone was dry.

A hysterical laugh bubbled up in Ceana, and she strangled it down. None of them would have chosen this path, but they were all here, drawn together. Salome, the former seelie fae, a selkie who'd laid down her immortal existence in exchange for being allowed to live and die as a human woman with Lord MacDonald. Lyall, the physician who'd worked so hard to save her when it seemed like life on land would kill her. Eachann, Lord MacDonald's guard, who'd chosen to honor their lifelong friendship even though he wanted nothing to do with the supernatural world.

And her and Gavran. The two peasants who'd gotten on the wrong side of a fairy, ended up cursed, and sought out Lady Salome MacDonald on the slim chance that the rumor she knew something about the fae was true.

None of them could have predicted it would go this far. Yet they'd all stayed together. Other than Gavran's family, she'd never known people willing to do that for each other. Maybe her experience of the world had been too small before to find the pockets of good still hidden throughout.

And now they had to face down one last monster to be free.

Eachann nudged his horse forward. They rode single file along the narrow path between the cliffs where Eliezer's cavern was hidden and the shoreline.

Gulls looped and screamed above, taking turns diving down to the waves. The sight was so natural it almost felt staged, like a play put on for them. She'd never take the mundane of each day for granted after this. Chopping neeps or mending would feel like a joy because no one would die if she didn't do it right.

The path opened up into the rolling hillside, and they spread their horses out rather than continuing to ride single file. She glanced behind her to where Gavran had been. He'd dropped his horse back to join Lyall. A snippet of their conversation floated to her. Gavran asking more questions, about stitching wounds this time.

She leaned back in her saddle. If she only focused on their voices and the briny smell of the sea and the cool breeze off the water taking the edge off the beating of the sun, she could imagine nothing stood between them and the future Gavran was dreaming of. Them married. Him apprenticing with Lyall. Her helping care for all the orphans running around Duntulm Castle, her brother among them.

Her eyes burned, and the muscles in her jaw clenched until her teeth ached. She couldn't look ahead like that. Not yet. It would hurt too much if they failed. She'd let Gavran do the dreaming for both of them. She had to keep her eyes on what they still had to do. Even peeking at what might be was too much of a distraction.

She maneuvered her horse up beside Salome's grey mare. "How do we find someone who's possessed?"

Saying the word sent a shiver down her arms. Maybe Gavran was the wiser of them, taking a moment of normalcy. Where was she to get the strength for what came next?

Salome's mare shook her head, chasing off the flies buzzing around them. "Our parish priest would know best."

A faint buzzing, not unlike the flies, started up in Ceana's head. "The parish priest? Not the one at Duntulm Castle?"

Salome nodded. "He and those under him know the people on our lands better than anyone else."

Aye, he surely did. He'd also remember her and Gavran as the ones he'd caught digging up graves not even a month past. He'd sworn to make them accountable for what they'd done. What were the chances he'd believe them if they tried to explain that they hadn't been grave-robbing? At least not in the way he'd assumed.

Though, perhaps that would be worse. They hadn't been looking for valuables, but they had been hoping to steal freshly dead flesh to lure out a monster. Even if the priest did believe them, they'd be hard-pressed to convince him that what they'd been doing had been in pursuit of good rather than evil.

And if he didn't believe them, he could raise the town against them. They might not wait for Lord MacDonald to execute what they'd see as justice. Even if they did, Lord MacDonald might not be able to save them. He'd have no proof to offer that they spoke the truth. And he couldn't reveal his and Salome's connection to the events. Ceana and Gavran had decided long ago that they wouldn't trade Salome and Lord MacDonald's lives for their own.

Bile burned at the back of her throat, and she swallowed hard. "Is there no one else who would be knowledgeable about rumored demon possession? A spaewife?"

"We haven't had a spaewife since Maeve left." Salome focused her piercing gaze on Ceana's face. "Why the hesitancy? We'll come up with something to tell him about why you're seeking out a person who's possessed."

Ceana poured out the rest of the story about when they'd gone to fight the nuckalevee. There'd been so many other more important things happening—like Gavran dying from poisonous nuckalevee venom—that their aborted grave-robbing hadn't come up. Eachann had helped them cut off Gavran's toe to lure out the nuckalevee, so Salome would have never had reason to think they'd tried anything else first.

Salome's face stayed peaceful throughout the tale. Her fingers running up and down her leather reins were the only hint of what might be going on inside.

Ceana had to force her gaze to stay on Salome's face rather than on the movement of her hands. It was as distracting as someone else's pacing might have been.

She ended her retelling. Salome sat silently.

The men's conversations around them suddenly seemed overly loud. Lord MacDonald and Eachann discussing guard rotations. Lyall recommending to Gavran that he practice stitching fabric to become familiar with using a needle. The swish and thwack of the horses' tails brushing back and forth against their sides.

"We have two options then." Salome's voice was soft.

Ceana edged her horse closer. "And those are?"

"You could travel to another parish. That leaves you without our aid should you need anything to complete the task the brollachan sets for you."

Ceana shook her head before Salome finished speaking. "We wouldn't have survived this long without your help."

"Then we can disguise your appearance. He saw you by lantern light, not daylight."

Ceana's skin tingled, and she tapped a fisted hand against her thigh. That seemed like a big risk. They'd need to change not only their appearance, but the way they moved and talked.

But she *had* tricked Brighde by disguising her appearance, and Brighde had seen her for longer than the priest had. It might work.

It would have to work.

～

CEANA'S FOOTSTEPS echoed off the stone floor of the church sanctuary. The sound seemed to bounce off the high ceilings and come back to her. Every word spoken in here would surely carry the same.

Including the priest's calls for help if he recognized them despite their transformations.

She pressed a hand to her hair and brought it back in front of her face. Her palm was still clean. None of the coloring was coming off at her touch. Salome and Duntulm Castle's chief cook had boiled together walnut leaves and chestnuts, then soaked her hair in it, turning her natural red into a muted brown. They'd assured her the color would stick. She'd need time and multiple washes before it would fade. Hopefully, her red hair was what the priest would remember most. With it gone, perhaps he wouldn't even think to associate her with the grave-robbers they'd been accused of being. She touched her hair again just to be sure.

"Stop doing that," Gavran whispered from where he limped beside her, practically dragging one foot along the stones, back hunched. "You're drawing attention to it."

Fair enough true. Were her hair nought but her hair, she wouldn't be fussing with it. She tugged the kerchief tied round it closer to her face and tightened the knot at her chin. "Aye, Dadaidh. You're right as always."

Maybe slipping into character now before they found the priest would help her remember.

Gavran made a face at her, but it didn't erase his smile. His skin was grubby with a layer of dust. It didn't quite create the wrinkles he would have had if he'd actually been her aged dadaidh, but it gave his skin an unhealthy pallor. Cook had used some other concoction to add mottling for age spots, and she'd sown tufts of gray horse hair to the close-fitted linen coif that swathed Gavran's entire head, hiding his actual hair. The coarse bits of horse hair stuck out in such a way that they looked like his own hair escaping. With the added hunch and limp, he was as well-hidden in plain sight as they could manage.

A large figure came through one of the side doors. The priest who they'd come to see.

He must have spotted them immediately because he strode in their direction. "Good morrow and blessings on you."

His gaze ran over them quickly. No flash of recognition or suspicion of any kind twisted his expression. His grin was wide and warm.

The knotted muscles in Ceana's shoulders and neck relaxed slightly.

"Good morrow, Athair." They'd decided to go with sprinkling in some Gaelic to hint that they might be traveling tinkers, but Gavran's voice also had a wobble and a creak to it as if he were as old as he was pretending to be. Perhaps he should have joined a group of troubadours and wandered around entertaining others for his meals. "We're needing some help if you can be providing it."

The priest stopped in front of them. His gaze flickered to Ceana and snagged for a moment. His eyebrows twitched downward slightly.

She dropped her own gaze. That seemed like the best way to appear modest and humble, but her heart beat double rhythm. A clammy feeling glazed over her skin. She was the one the priest got the best look at that night. Perhaps they should have tried to disguise her as an old woman as well.

She peeked up. The priest had returned his attention to Gavran.

"I'm at your service," he said, "if it be the will of the Lord. What can I do for you?"

"My brathair's near to going to be with the Almighty." Gavran tapped his walking stick lightly on the floor. "Years ago, his only child went astray and left home. We're hoping to reunite them before he passes."

Ceana's fingers twitched with the desire to touch her hair again. She tangled them in her skirt instead. This was the challenging moment. They'd had to carefully choose their words so that they didn't say whether they were looking for a man or a woman. For if they guessed wrong about the gender of a potentially possessed person in the parish, the priest would send them away and they'd be none the wiser that they'd missed their chance.

The priest nodded along like every word mattered. But he offered nothing. A good quality for someone who needed to carefully listen to confessions, but not helpful to them now.

Gavran wrapped his other hand around his walking stick. "Will you help us?"

The priest tapped a finger against his lips. His gaze came back to Ceana. "You're not from Duntulm? When I first saw you, I thought you looked familiar."

Ceana's mouth went dry. If she spoke, would he recognize her voice? She'd called out to Gavran that night, telling him to get out of the grave.

Gavran rapped his stick again, and the priest looked back at him. "We wouldn't need your help if we knew where to find the prodigal. But my nighean here looks a little like my brathair's child."

Ceana held back a flinch. They'd lost every chance if the person they sought happened to be blond and broad of shoulder.

The priest squinted and leaned forward slightly toward Ceana. "You'll have to forgive me. It must be too many hours working by lantern light have left my eyes weaker than they used to be. Perhaps if you gave me a name, I could tell you if we've anyone here who answers to it."

Gavran's mouth drooped open slightly.

Christ preserve them. They had no name to give. And Gavran clearly didn't know what to say in response.

An idea flitted into her mind. But it would mean she'd have to speak. She could only pray her voice wouldn't be recognized. She tried to pitch it deeper to be safe. "We're not sure what name my cousin uses now. A demon…"

She forced her words to choke off as if it were too difficult to say more. It wasn't hard. The idea of speaking to someone who was demon possessed *did* make her throat try to close.

The priest's eyebrows moved together again. "Ah, aye. You need say no more. I don't know what name she once went by, but she calls herself Caillic now." He glanced around the empty sanctuary. "She's a little hard to find. I'll take you myself."

Ceana sneaked a look at Gavran. There wasn't any good reason she could think of not to let the priest guide them, other than that the longer he spent with them, the more likely he was to realize they weren't who they were pretending to be. But that certainly wasn't a reason she could give for leaving the priest behind. Gavran lifted one shoulder in a what-can-we-do shrug.

"That's more than kind of you, Athair," he said.

The priest's neck reddened. "Nay, nay. Let me gather provisions for us. It's half a morning's walk."

He was going to provide them with food as well? Ceana's jaw muscles tightened. This was a good man of God. And they were lying to him and deceiving him. In the house of the Lord no less. It was sheer grace they hadn't been struck down already. But maybe the Almighty was showing compassion because saving her brother's life once the curses were removed from her was more important than telling falsehoods to a priest. She couldn't see a way to achieve the one without also committing the other.

The priest marched off, his forceful gait a little faster than Ceana had seen from him before.

A frown crept across Gavran's face. "Why do you think my thanks embarrassed him?"

Ceana pulled herself out of her thoughts. Gavran stood watching where the priest had disappeared through a door. He hadn't dropped character, but his eyes were narrowed.

"What do you mean?" Her words bounced around the room even though she'd tried to keep them quiet.

Gavran motioned her back toward the door. They stopped just inside where the priest could still easily spot them, but the sound wouldn't resonate as much. Hopefully.

He motioned vaguely toward his face. "He seemed uncomfortable with my simple expression of gratitude."

Ceana bit down on her lower lip. The priest had nearly blushed when Gavran thanked him. No man was that humble. Not even a priest. But if it wasn't humility, what was it? Guilt? If so, they were in trouble.

She grabbed Gavran's sleeve and tugged toward the door. "We need to leave."

CHAPTER 4

*G*avran held firm. He raised his eyebrows. "You're going to need to give me a reason. It'll be near impossible finding this Caillic without him."

Her blood singed through her veins, hot and urgent. "We won't be able to find her at all if we're locked up or dead. He's gone to get help to capture and punish us, not food. He must have recognized me."

Gavran angled toward her and placed both hands on her upper arms. He rubbed gently.

The spots where he touched calmed, like water settling down from a boil.

"I was only letting you know something I noticed that we should be aware of. But if we panic and run, we miss our best chance. I think we should stay."

She shifted her weight from left to right. Gavran might be right. But what if he wasn't. Wasn't it better they acted now rather than waiting and gambling?

She drew in a long breath. Or was that her time spent under the curses talking again? When she'd had to act without thinking in the hopes of getting out in front of the curses for even a second. How was she to know?

Gavran watched her calmly, his eyes the loch blue that she loved so much. It was like he carried the peacefulness of the water inside him compared to her rough storms.

The banshee had warned her that she needed to stop thinking she was the one who always knew best or she'd lose what mattered most to her. Maybe that caution carried weigh for more than just their fight with the baobhan sith.

Trust simply didn't come naturally. Even with Gavran. It felt like a colony of ants was trying to burrow out from under her skin.

But they had no hope of a future even with the curses removed if she couldn't find a way to meet him partway. If she couldn't find a way to start letting go of the ways she'd had to act to survive that weren't healthy for a normal life.

She leaned her forehead against his shoulder. "Alright. We wait."

A door at the back of the sanctuary creaked. They broke apart. Ceana tensed.

Only the priest carrying a rough cloth sack came through the door. No townsfolk with pitchforks. No guard from MacDonald castle that had been rounded up from the tavern.

Gavran had been right about them waiting. She would have tossed away their best chance out of impulsive fear.

The priest led them through the streets of Duntulm, his boots making a squelching sound any time one of his steps accidentally found a puddle of pig manure rather than the regular earthen street. The yeasty scent of fresh bread and the smokiness of the blacksmith's forge warred with the stinging bite of sunbaked urine as they meandered past homes and businesses.

The slow pace the priest presumably kept for Gavran's sake— believing him to be an old man—was made even slower by all the people who greeted the priest. Clearly this man wasn't like the one she remembered from Dunvegan, who'd always seemed to be looking down at her family and wishing they were someone else's problem.

This priest pulled an apple from his bag and gave it to a child who ran up to him. He promised a visit to an elderly woman. He knew each of them by name.

What might have been different if she'd lived someplace like this? Could a priest like this have gotten through to her dadaidh? She shook her head. Nay, no good could come of playing that game. The more she dwelled back there, the more she wished for something that hadn't been, the less she could focus on what was in front of her. She'd need every drop of energy and attention she had for their conversation with the brollachan. She couldn't change how things had been with her dadaidh, but she still had a chance to change how her future would play out.

They finally passed the outskirts of the town and headed down a dirt path that took them in the opposite direction from Duntulm Castle and the sea. The grass was higher on this side of town, as if fewer people regularly came this way, even to graze their sheep.

If she let herself, her mind could make up all sorts of terrifying reasons for the difference, but she wouldn't let herself. It wasn't that animals sensed the evil of the brollachan and refused to come this way. It wasn't that the brollachan's relatives came to visit it, and so travelers were more vulnerable this way. It wasn't that—

Ack. She clearly needed more practice at keeping her imagination in check.

The priest shot her that furtive look again. Was he still trying to figure out if he'd seen her before? They were far enough from town now that she and Gavran could likely escape even if he figured it out. Unless he'd planned an ambush for them instead when he'd claimed to be packing supplies.

Tears built behind her eyes, and she blinked hard against

them. Would she ever be able to stop thinking the worst at every turn?

"I know what you're thinking." The priest's voice was loud even though he seemed to be trying to soften it. "I'd be wondering the same thing."

Hopefully the priest had no idea what she was thinking. Though it was possible if he did that he'd be wondering exactly what kind of *eejits* threw themselves into the path of yet another monster? It'd all be worth it in the end. If they survived.

But since it wasn't that, what in all the green isle was he talking about?

She glanced at Gavran. His head moved in her direction, but he couldn't seem to meet her gaze while also staying hunched over like an old man. His shuffling feet kicked up a fresh puff of dust with each dragging movement.

"What do you speak of, Athair?" Gavran asked, the gravelly shake of his voice so convincing she might not have recognized the voice as his had she not been looking at him.

The priest kept his stride steady and his eyes focused ahead of them. Almost as if he were too ashamed to meet their eyes. "I did try to exorcize the demon from Caillic when she first moved onto MacDonald lands." Red crept up his neck again and bled into his ears. "I'd never leave someone in that state if I could help. I wasn't able to. The host is willing. She wants the demon. I wanted to warn you since you've come wanting to take her home with you. She might not be willing to go, and if she does, it might cause you more trouble than you planned."

His words came out fast as if he wanted to be rid of them. Even when he finished, he didn't turn to look in their direction.

So that was the cause of the guilt and embarrassment Gavran had noticed earlier from the priest. Not that the priest planned to betray them, but that he felt he'd failed Caillic's family. If they had been her family, Ceana would have been grateful for his explanation.

Now she only felt worse. And full of even more questions. She'd seen evil up close, in both human form and in the unseelie. "Why would anyone want that?"

She flinched. She'd forgotten to deepen her voice the way she had earlier.

The priest's gaze was focused elsewhere. He didn't appear to have even noticed. "She earns her living telling fortunes."

Was that the brollachan lying to the man? Salome had told them more than once that the fae weren't all-knowing. They couldn't read minds or know the future. But she couldn't say that to the priest. "I was always taught only the Almighty knows the future."

The first smile since they'd left the borders of Duntulm cracked the man's face. It fell away again almost immediately. "Aye. That's the truth. But we have to remember that the evil one delights in lies and tricks and confusion. He and his servants have been around since before man was created. They've seen more than any single man can imagine. With that much knowledge, their guesses often come close enough that they seem to have the ability to predict the future. Enough that people pay her good coin to do it, anyway."

A bead of cold sweat ran down the back of Ceana's neck. The banshee had said something similar about how long she'd lived and how much she'd seen and the advantage that gave to the unseelie fae.

She swung her hand so that her fingers brushed against Gavran's. They were like children playing a game of chase with an adult in approaching the brollachan. Especially, it seemed, this brollachan. If it enjoyed predicting the future, it likely knew the fairy they sought. But it would surely only tell them if doing so benefitted it rather than them. It was a game they'd only be allowed to play because the brollachan desired it.

The priest pointed to a wattle-and-daub cottage with a

thatched roof hunched beneath a cluster of ash trees. "That's her home."

No tendril of smoke came from the house. Even in summer, she should have had a fire for cooking. Perhaps Caillic no longer lived here.

A heavy weight settled in Ceana's chest, and she slowed her steps. Caillic needed to live here. Caillic needed to be exactly what they were expecting and hoping her to be. Otherwise the life Ceana wanted was forfeit. The cursed wishes would stay in place. And in the end that would be worse. She was just so tired.

She slowed her pace to match Gavran's.

The priest glanced between them. "I'll go in with you. Perhaps together we can reason with her. And I'll pray daily that once she's back among family, she'll no longer wish to consort with demons."

Gavran glanced up at her through his horse-hair fringe. She gave a tiny shake of her head in return. They couldn't allow the priest to go in with them. If Caillic were in control at the moment, she wouldn't recognize them and their lie would be revealed. If the demon were in control, any number of horrible things could happen, all of which would put the lie to their story.

Gavran straightened himself slightly. "It'll be better we go alone. Surely bringing a priest to her home will only anger her."

The priest's gaze slid over Gavran's hunched form. "Demons can make even the calmest of people wild and dangerous. My conscience won't allow me to send you in alone."

Ceana barely restrained herself from kicking at a stick along the path. They couldn't exactly stop the priest. Two of her together wouldn't have matched his size. Even together with Gavran, they were likely outmatched. Not to mention that *her* conscience wouldn't allow her to abuse a man of God. Surely the Almighty wouldn't look kindly on that, regardless of her excuse. Besides, if they knocked him out, they'd only be in more trouble once he awoke.

A few more strides and they'd be at the brollachan's door.

She stopped and spun around. Dust kicked up in a little cloud at her feet. The priest stuttered to a stop facing her, his mouth forming an O. Gavran shot her a look that clearly said *what are you doing?*

She gave him a little shrug. She needed to speak now. The priest and Gavran were both watching her. Maybe if she told him a version of the truth? But what would that be? That they were here to make a deal with a demon? She couldn't say that to a priest. Just the thought of the words left a stale taste in her mouth. There was no way she could say that without sounding like they were willing to blink at evil for their own benefit.

Isn't that what you're doing? a tiny accusatory voice whispered in her head.

The three of them stared at each other. The priest's eyebrows drew down, and he tilted his head to one side as if trying to work out what was happening.

The door to the cottage creaked open.

Ceana turned back around so quickly she almost lost her balance.

Shadows from the trees above cast the woman in the doorway half into shadows. Her hair was entirely hidden under a cream-colored kerchief tied around her head. Shadows ringed her eyes, and her features were long and narrow, stretched out in a way that not even malnutrition could produce. If the priest remembered Gavran's excuse earlier that Ceana looked familiar because she and her "cousin" had similar features, he'd no doubt sense a lie. Nothing about them matched.

A haze seemed to surround the woman.

Had dust gotten into her eyes and was making them water? Ceana blinked rapidly. The image didn't clear, but it was less a haze and more a sense of seeing double. Like two people stood in one place and sometimes their edges weren't perfectly aligned.

Caillic turned her gaze to the priest. "There's nothing for you here, servant of the Almighty. You should spend your time with those whose souls are still saveable."

Cold dripped down into Ceana's core. Nothing about the woman's voice was strange or unearthly. It wasn't unnaturally deep or resonant. But that was surely the brollachan speaking, though she couldn't have said what about it made her certain if she'd been asked.

The priest took a large step forward. He stopped in line with Ceana. "All souls are saveable until death claims them. It's time you let go of this woman."

Ceana sneaked a glance at him. His tone was so firm and determined, as if this were a battle he'd had before and would willingly continue having as long as it took. He believed what he said.

One half of Caillic's mouth twisted up. She didn't reply. The priest had said earlier that Caillic welcomed the demon. Perhaps that's why the brollachan said nothing.

Her gaze slid to Ceana. Her lips flattened into a hard line. "I know you."

The priest took another step forward, almost the way someone would approach an angry bull they were trying to subdue. Slightly sidelong, hoping the animal wouldn't notice. "Your family is here to take you home."

Her eyes went dark—there and gone, so quickly Ceana couldn't be sure it hadn't been a trick of the light. "They're not my family. They slaughtered my family."

CHAPTER 5

"Christ preserve us." Gavran whispered the words in the tone of a desperate prayer.

The priest shot a look his direction. Ceana stiffened, every muscle in her body suddenly rigid. This must be what a rabbit felt like when cornered by a fox on one side and a hunter on the other. Gavran had spoken in his own voice, not the voice he'd created for the character of the old man he was pretending to be. There'd be no maintaining the ruse now, especially not alongside Caillic's accusation.

The priest shifted slightly, almost as if he were trying to keep them and Caillic in his sights at once. A thin line of sweat broke out on his brow. "What does she mean by that? What's going on here?"

Gavran glanced at Ceana, then brought himself up to his proper height and met the priest's gaze. He pressed a hand into his lower back, as if hunching over for so long had stiffened his muscles. "We're not actually her family."

"I gathered that much." The priest leaned forward slightly, squinting at Ceana. "The grave-robbers. That's why I know your face." His tone was cold now. "What's the true reason you wanted me to bring you here? Did you think a woman possessed would be easy prey for thieves like yourselves?"

Her mouth went as dry as if she'd eaten a mouthful of the dust at her feet. Had she wanted to steal from someone, a person possessed by a brollachan wouldn't have been her first choice. She'd likely be physically stronger than a normal woman.

But what could she tell him? They weren't here to try to free Caillic from the brollachan, which was likely the only purpose the priest would support. She couldn't even lie and say they were. The brollachan wouldn't speak to them if they claimed to be there to exorcise it.

"We did dig up a grave, but it wasn't for our own gain." Gavran's voice was firm and confident, as if he wasn't having the same inner battle she was. "We needed to lure a monster and kill it." He motioned towards Caillic. "The creature possessing her considered the monster family." Gavran finally looked in Ceana's direction. He shrugged. "The truth seemed like the best option."

The priest placed himself between them and Caillic. "I can't allow you to kill her. Killing her won't kill the demon, and the woman will lose her chance to repent and find salvation."

Ceana's throat tightened. Of all the reactions the priest could have had to their declaration, his first concern had been about the eternal destiny of Caillic. He hadn't doubted that they were fighting supernatural beings. He believed in the battle between good and evil that happened where humans weren't able to see it. And he was willing to place himself as a shield in the middle of it to try to spare one woman whose soul was still lost and give her more time. This priest had taken orders from a true faith and not from selfish motivations.

Which in a way was unfortunate for them. Had he been self-ishly motivated, they might have been able to bribe him to look the other way. A wry smile twisted her lips. "We're not here to kill her. We have a different mission."

What she wouldn't have given to be able to pass him Lord

MacDonald's name. To send him to speak with Salome. But she couldn't reveal their involvement, especially not in front of the brollachan. It'd be a death sentence for them.

"I'm not the one you should fear for, servant of the Most High." Caillic's voice was so smooth it was almost oily. "Fear for them. I have a score to settle."

Something flickered across the priest's face as if he realized for the first time that he'd accidentally gotten himself in the middle of something he didn't fully understand. But he didn't move.

"You need to leave now, Father," Gavran said. "Please."

Ceana's gaze snapped to Gavran. When had he learned to have that sort of confidence and command in his voice? Calm, aye. He'd always been calm. But this was something more. Something that hadn't been there before they'd survived the baobhan sith.

The priest looked between them. "You give your word you won't kill her?"

Caillic chuckled as if even the idea that they might be able to was laughable.

Gavran placed a hand over his heart as if taking a pledge of loyalty, his gaze not shifting in Caillic's direction. "I give my word."

The priest frowned. "I'll return to check on her. If you break your vow, I'll make sure the whole town knows to be on watch for you. I'll report it to Lord MacDonald as well. There won't be anywhere on MacDonald lands you'll be able to hide."

If they murdered a human being, not even Salome and Lord MacDonald would be able to protect them. Nor should they. She'd only escaped punishment for killing Hugh because it'd been in self-defence.

The priest headed back down the path that had brought them here. He looked back multiple times before he was out of sight.

And then they were alone with the brollachan.

~

GAVRAN CLENCHED his teeth to keep from calling out after the priest to stay. Somehow his presence had felt like the only thing holding the brollachan in check. But they needed to let the man go before they could make their deal with the brollachan. They had to do this on their own.

He took a step closer to Caillic the way the priest had done. The man had more experience with her than they did. Imitating him seemed like a reasonable first step. "May we come inside? We'd like to speak to you."

Caillic's gaze ran slowly and invasively over him, then over Ceana. "There was a time when I'd have welcomed you both in, but you're no use to me now. I can inhabit this body, but I can't feel its pleasures."

Caillic's cheek twitched slightly. Something about the motion made Gavran think the brollachan wanted to curse the Almighty for what had happened to it, but it wasn't able to blaspheme against its creator.

Caillic licked her lips. Her fingers played over the *sgian* she wore openly at her waist. "I could tell your future, if you like. In fact, I'll do it now." Her voice deepened in a way that somehow carried a feeling of rolling thunder. "It's full of blood."

She yanked the *sgian* from its sheath and whipped it at them.

Gavran shoved Ceana to the side. A burning line seared across his cheek, and a thwack of the *sgian* lodging in wood came from far behind him. He raised his hand to his face. His fingers came away coated in blood. An inch closer, and the *sgian* would have lodged in him instead of the tree.

A desire for home flooded through him. The peacefulness of taking the sheep out to graze. The moist, earthly smell of the freshly turned soil as he prepared the ground for planting. No monsters wanting their toes or their blood or some other part of them.

Ceana had raised herself up onto all fours. She glared at him. "*Eejit.* She could have killed you."

An ache filled his chest. Aye, at home he'd had all those things, but he hadn't had Ceana, not since the wishes. Even angry, she was beautiful. "Better than her killing you."

Her mouth twitched in the way it did when she was fighting a smile. She clambered to her feet and pressed her sleeve against the cut. "Better she kill neither of us."

"That's one promise I can't make," Caillic said, the unnaturally deep rumble still in her voice. "I can promise I'll make you suffer first. Does that help?"

Ceana whirled toward her. The darkness of her expression matched the thunder in Caillic's voice. Whatever she was about to say to the brollachan, it wasn't going to get them what they wanted. They had to move more carefully around the brollachan than they would an angry skunk.

Gavran grabbed Ceana's hand and tugged her back into his side. She connected with him and let out a tiny *oof*. "We came to bargain, but if you'd rather make threats, we can leave."

Caillic's smile was nasty. "Come to make a deal with the devil, have you? No wonder you sent the other one away."

Gavran stomach turned over. Was that what they were doing? Right and wrong had been so much easier to figure out before Ceana had come back into his life. But that might have been because the wishes made sure he stayed happy and blinded him to any true ills and evils in the world. Now things no longer seemed to slide as easily into one category or another. Dealing with the brollachan would have surely been wrong had they been doing it to try to gather wealth for themselves, but curing the wishes was different, wasn't it?

Or had they already crossed the line and were so deep in that they couldn't even tell right from wrong anymore? He couldn't even blame the nuckalevee venom now. His actions were his own again, and he'd be responsible for any choice he made.

"Not with the devil," Ceana said from beside him quietly as if she'd been able to read his thoughts on his face. "And only to right a wrong."

"You want to right a wrong?" Caillic's voice boomed, unnaturally loud. "What about the wrong you committed in slaying my brethren?"

A shudder ran over Gavran's body. There was an ancientness to her voice. They'd surely made a mistake in coming here. Might they not have reached the point where it was no longer worth the cost of continuing to try to cure the wishes?

"That was righting a wrong." Ceana practically spit the words at the brollachan. If she'd been a dog, her fangs would have been bared. "The nuckalevee had taken life after life, so we took its life."

His muscles tensed. They shouldn't irritate this creature. It couldn't take physical form anymore, but that didn't mean it was without some powers still.

Ceana had moved closer to the brollachan. He put his hands on her arms and drew her back towards him. He pressed his lips close to her ear. "This isn't the fairy who cursed you. Maybe you should save your anger for her, and not keep poking with a stick the one you need to guide you to her."

"A life for a life, is it?" Caillic swept a hand in the direction of the open door of her cottage. "Then I know the terms I'll ask for. And I won't barter. All that remains is to see if what you're asking is something I can provide."

Caillic disappeared inside her cottage, leaving her door hanging open.

Ceana glared after her, features tight, a stain of red across her cheeks. Her jaw flexed and released.

The back of his neck prickled with that sense he sometimes got of something he shouldn't be able to know about her. Like the memories of their true past together pushed against the barrier of the wishes, wanting to break free. To tell him that she might look angry, but she was actually trying not to cry. To tell him that her anger was a cover, a way for her not to show a different emotion that she'd always been taught was weak.

He turned her around so she faced him, but kept his hands on her arms. He tilted his head in the direction of Caillic's cottage. "Now that's a trap if I ever saw one, don't you think?" He made sure his tone was clearly teasing, so she wouldn't misunderstand and think he was criticizing her for earlier.

Ceana snorted, loud and unladylike. Her eyes widened and then a laugh peeled from her lips—the one he loved that sounded like church bells. But it shifted into sobs that shook her body. He pulled her tight against him.

If they made it through this, he'd make sure she had as many days as possible of rest and happiness as were within his power to give her.

Her sniffling calmed, and she drew back. She wiped at her cheeks. "More likely to be a trap than the one I spotted earlier. But everything will like as not seem like a trap to us until we can stay far away from unseelie."

Lord hear their prayer for that and grant it.

He took her hand. They'd didn't actually need to discuss whether or not to go into Caillic's cottage. They'd come here to barter. They couldn't walk away without knowing if she was going to actually offer them a deal and if it'd be one they could live with.

He glanced down at Ceana. *A life for a life*, Caillic had said. That was a path they'd walked before when they'd needed fresh human flesh to lure the nuckalevee. Caillic might very well ask for something they weren't willing to give. They wouldn't kill each other, nor would they kill another human being.

An ache wrapped around his heart and pulsed with every beat. Memories of the times in the past when Ceana had thought she'd reached a dead end flashed across his vision, practically blinding him. His *sgian* in her hands as she attempted to plunge it into her owns stomach. A shattered tea cup once full of poison on the ground.

His mouth went dry. Surely she'd changed enough in what they'd undergone to know that her life mattered too much to cast it aside in pursuit of this quest. If they failed, he'd find a way to make life worth living for her, even under the wishes.

He squeezed her hand, needing to feel the warmth and strength in her fingers tighter in his. Her eyes flickered down, and she returned the pressure.

She looked up at him and mouthed, *Together*.

They stopped just outside the threshold of Caillic's cottage. The interior was dark. No fire in the hearth. No lantern. Not even a candle. Only the light coming in the door and the small, high windows lit the room, leaving it dim.

He shaded his eyes from the outside light, and shapes started to make sense. The hulking mass in the center of the room as a table. The pile to the side was bedding.

Caillic sat at the table. "You don't want to bore me. Bore me and I'll kill you instead of offering you my compromise."

Ceana strode into the room, head up as if she weren't going into the lair of yet another monster.

Gavran's throat tightened. He swallowed against it and followed her. Sometimes she was brave to the point of foolish. And he loved even that about her.

Ceana sat across the table from Caillic without waiting for an invitation. He couldn't bring himself to sit as well. One of them had to be ready in case Caillic attacked. He couldn't react as quickly sitting down as he could standing. He placed himself behind Ceana's right shoulder instead.

Caillic picked up a piece of what looked like raw fish from a plate and swallowed it without chewing. "What is it you want? Spit it out before I change my mind about treating with you."

Ceana fisted her hands in her lap. "The name of the fairy who gave us three wishes. We know that your kind keeps track of interactions between humans and the fae."

Caillic slurped down another sliver of fish. Gavran gagged slightly and tamped the reflex down.

Her gaze shifted to him. She pushed the plate slightly in his direction. "Would you like some?" Her smile was mocking, as if she were daring him.

Ceana would have taken the dare, and she would have been able to somehow keep the raw meat down. His stomach pitched at the thought. He'd only make an *eejit* of himself by trying. And he'd risk insulting Caillic by not. The brollachan's game had begun.

Ceana pushed the plate back towards Caillic with the tips of two of her fingers. "Nothing comes for free, and we'd rather only pay for what we came here for."

"It seems what I've heard about you isn't wrong." Caillic moved the strips of flesh around her plate with a finger, but she didn't take another. "We have a deal. You will free an enslaved kelpie for me. In exchange, I will give you information."

A kelpie. The words didn't want to sink into Gavran's mind. How was it possible that they kept having to deal with horse-like creatures? At least this time he was guaranteed not to have to ride it. That was certain death with a kelpie. Climb astride and it'd pull you down into the nearest lake and eat all of you except your liver.

"What do you mean by *free a kelpie*?" Ceana asked. "We're mortals. We can't travel to Tartaros and let your kind free." She opened her mouth as if she were about to say more. Instead, she shot him a swift glance, snapped her mouth shut, and bit down on her bottom lip like she needed help keeping the words in.

"You took one of my family from this world. It seems only fair you return one to it." Caillic smiled, but the movement wasn't quite right. Like she was a puppet and someone was pulling the strings to make her lips and teeth form a mimicry of a smile. "A life for a life, you said. Your terms, not mine."

Ceana stiffened.

He brushed his hand against her back. "Be more specific, please. We won't agree to an impossible bargain."

Caillic speared a piece of flesh with one long fingernail, but she didn't eat it. She merely held it aloft like a trophy. "A kelpie is being held captive near here. A human man managed to get a bridle onto him, and now my unseelie brethren is a slave. The human uses him to build his own wealth. I want you to free him. It's as simple as that. And it's not much to ask considering what you've done in the past, now is it?"

CHAPTER 6

$\mathcal{T}$he outbuildings of the manor belonging to the man who supposedly held the kelpie captive was the largest grouping of buildings Ceana had ever seen apart from a castle or a village. Barns circled out from the center, each letting off the distinctive warm, acrid scent and buzz of flies that came along with livestock. Men passed in and out, hauling barrows full of manure. Unlike the men who fulfilled the same role at Duntulm Castle, these weren't tossing jokes back and forth about dung, nor were they competing to see who could wheel the fullest barrow or complete a loop fastest. Instead, they worked in silence, faces unsmiling and shoulders hunched.

The house itself could have fit four or more of the cottages she'd grown up in inside of it. The smell of roasting meat wafted from a building nearby. Ceana's mouth watered, and she swallowed. Even if their ploy worked and they were hired on as laborers, that wouldn't be for them.

Near the house, masons chiseled away at large stones. "Is he building himself a wall?"

Gavran shrugged, but his head swivelled left and right, taking it all in.

A knot formed at the base of her throat. Walls were only built during times of threat, and usually non-lords put up palisades made from trees. A stone wall was permanent. It wasn't something he should be expending the resources to build at any time, let alone during the peace they currently had on the isle.

Not unless his control of the kelpie had given him grander ideas. Perhaps even of challenging the MacLeods, MacDonalds, or Mackinnons for power. Of making himself a lord alongside them. Such a coup could throw the entire isle into chaos and bloodshed.

Gavran's fingers brushed her elbow. "We'll have to ask someone where to find the master." He raised his hand in the direction of a man heading toward the kitchen with a bow slung over one shoulder and a brace of dead pigeons over the other. "Hail, fellow."

The man stopped and raised a hand to shade his eyes. "What can I do for you?"

"My wife and I are looking for work." Gavran clasped his hands deferentially in front of him. "Where can we find your master to present ourselves?"

The lie seemed to slip easily off of Gavran's tongue. Maybe because he wished they were already wed.

The man glanced between them.

For once at least, they shouldn't be turned away on their appearance alone. When they'd gone back to Duntulm Castle after their meeting with the brollachan, Salome had made sure they both had clothes that were new and sturdy but not so fine that they'd draw unwanted attention as they traveled.

"I'm not sure the master's needing any more hands."

There was something underneath his words and the way he glanced at her again. Ceana couldn't quite pick it out. Not unfriendliness. Warning? But why would he be trying to warn them away?

A gruesome idea flitted across her mind of the master feeding servants to the kelpie to keep it docile, but that was ridiculous. He wouldn't have been able to get away with that practice for any length of time before rumors spread. A household with that sort of tale attached to it wouldn't be as lively as this one, no matter what wages the master offered to make up for it. Coin was of little use if you were dead and couldn't spend it.

Gavran smiled openly at the man. Either he hadn't caught what she had in the other man's tone or he was pretending he hadn't.

"We're willing to work anywhere we're needed," Gavran said. "I've tended sheep. My wife has experience in the kitchens and mending nets."

The man's gaze slid to Ceana again. His sun-weathered features made it difficult to tell if he looked sad or annoyed. "I've heard Duntulm Castle is a fine place for men with wives. Have you tried there yet?"

Ceana's mouth went so dry that her lips felt like they'd crack from lack of moisture. Some masters and lords felt it was their right to bed women within their household, even ones who already had husbands. Was that what this man was trying to warn them of? In many a way, that was as bad as secretly feeding his servants to the kelpie.

"Aye, we've been." Gavran did a good job of making his voice sound regretful. "They've no need of additional hands either. We'd like to talk to the master about a position if we could. Might be he can find something for us."

The man's shoulders slumped, and he sighed. "Master Budge is working the west field."

The look he shot them as he turned away clearly said *I did try to warn you.*

She and Gavran made their way through the cluster of buildings towards the west side of the settlement. "Do you get the sense Budge isn't a good master?"

The line of Gavran's jaw hardened. "Were we what we

pretended to be, I wouldn't stay. Better a dish of vegetables where there is love, as the Holy Scripture says. I wouldn't risk you around a master like Budge even if it meant all we had to fill our bellies was a handful of foraged mushrooms."

She looked around to make sure no one was paying them any attention, then popped up on her toes, and brushed her lips against his. The hard lines in his face softened slightly.

She looked into each outbuilding as they passed until she located the stable where the horses were kept. "Do you think they'll keep it with the other horses?" she whispered.

Gavran followed her gaze. "I think they'd have to. Wouldn't it raise questions if they kept one horse stabled on its own?" He frowned. "Will it look just like any other horse, do you think?"

"I imagine so. We'd have heard rumors otherwise."

And, according to her mamaidh's stories, the kelpie's likeness to any other horse was how it was able to lure foolish travelers onto its back. If it looked supernatural at all, it wouldn't be able to trick its prey.

Gavran veered wide, giving two horses tethered to the side of a wagon enough space that the wagon itself could have fit between him and them. "How will we know then? It could be any of them."

The kelpie would be able to speak if it chose. But if it didn't, they wouldn't be able to identify it that way. "We might have to take the halters off every horse in the stable if that's what's allowing him to control it."

And hope they could get the job done without being caught.

They followed the path that had been trodden down in the tall grasses on the west side of the settlement. The breeze made the grass sway like water.

Gavran stopped and shot an arm out in front of her. He pointed. The black-and-white dappled body of an adder disappeared into the longer grasses from where it must have been napping in the sun on the path before it felt the vibrations of their footsteps. They let it disappear and continued on their way.

Ceana glanced back at the snake's path. What she wouldn't give to go back to the days when accidentally stepping on an adder in the grass had been her biggest fear.

The long grass stopped suddenly. Off to one side of the path, three men swung sickles, laying out the grass to dry for hay.

"We're looking for Master Budge," Gavran called out.

One man lowered his sickle and mopped a sleeve over his brow. "You're headed the right way. He's past that far line of trees. But the master likes to work alone. Unless you have an urgent message, you're better off waiting at the main house."

The man turned back to his work.

No matter. There could be no misunderstanding his directions. The line of trees was the only one as far as she could see. All the others seemed to have long been cleared for grazing pastures and fields.

Gavran ran a finger over his upper lip. "He not only works the fields instead of having servants do the hard labor, but he prefers to do it himself."

She should have picked up on the strangeness of it. "You think he's working the kelpie now?"

The brollachan had said all they needed to do to free the kelpie was remove its bridle. They might be finished with this task and headed back before the sun set. A few hours, another unpleasant conversation with the brollachan, and she could shed the curses like a cloak on an overly hot day. She could almost feel her shoulders lighten. She spun on her heel and headed down the path in the indicated direction, walking as quickly as she could without looking suspicious to the men cutting grass.

Gavran hurried up behind her and caught her arm. "We're taking a risk if we interrupt him. He must not want anyone seeing what the kelpie can do. He won't hire us if he thinks we spotted anything. He'll want to get rid of us before we can put enough pieces together to suspect anything strange."

Instead of letting him pull her to a stop, she kept on walking. He was forced to let her go and fall into step beside her.

"We don't need to be hired if we can get the bridle off it now. Budge is alone. You can distract or overpower him while I remove the bridle. It'll be easier than we expected."

Gavran snorted. "When has anything ever been easier than we expected."

She scowled at him. Fair point, but he didn't need to make it. She was trying not to expect death and doom every time she blinked. "Aren't you supposed to be the one who thinks the best?"

Gavran snorted again, but it had the edge of a chuckle to it.

They went the rest of the way in silence. The copse of trees was thick enough with scrub that she couldn't see through it. Voices carried to her before she could see who was beyond them.

"I thought he said Budge liked to work alone," Gavran whispered.

Aye, the field worker had indeed said that. She strained her ears. The tone of the voices carried tension. One sounded angry and the other scared.

Gavran motioned for her to leave the path. They crept up to the treeline through the tall grass. It tickled her arms, and she set each foot down carefully in case another adder had taken shelter in the grass at their approach.

The voices took shape the closer she got. One sounded young. Either a girl or a boy whose voice hadn't shifted into that of a man's yet.

"You're acting like a bairn," a man's voice said. "You've nothing to fear."

"But mamaidh said—"

"I don't care what your mamaidh said. She doesn't know what she's talking about. I'll remind her to keep her mouth shut later. Get over here."

Budge and his son then.

Ceana gently parted the brush and leaned closer. Gavran came in beside her.

The ground on the other side was rocky. At a glance she would have said it was unsuitable for growing anything. At best, he could have grazed sheep there. But a horse nearly as well-muscled as a bull and tall as she'd ever seen stood in the middle of a clearing, its harness tethered to a rock that should have been too heavy for it to move.

Yet the drag marks behind the boulder indicated it'd been doing exactly that.

He was using the kelpie to clear ground that should have been useless.

She leaned farther into the bushes. The kelpie was supposed to look like any other horse, but something wasn't right. His edges seemed almost blurred, like she was looking at him through tears.

The kelpie turned its head in her direction, almost as if it could sense her watching. For a second, she was staring into the skinless face and unearthly golden eye of the nuckalevee again. Her breath hitched. She blinked hard, and the memory passed.

The creature that looked at her from across the field now had the normal soft brown eyes of a regular horse. The gentle gaze of the horses at Duntulm Castle had always calmed her, even while they were preparing for something awful. But this time she couldn't shake the sense that it was a mask. Like a thief who smiled at you while preparing to cut your purse strings and stab you in the gut for extra measure.

Something cold slithered down her throat and wrapped around her heart. How could it look so innocent if something evil lurked beneath? And yet it still made her want to draw back, crawl under the bushes, and hide until she was sure it was gone. A push and a pull.

Gavran leaned close to her, his lips nearly touching her skin.

A pleasant shiver ran down her, but even it couldn't completely erase the clamminess building on the back of her neck.

"How can we be sure it's the kelpie?" His words were so soft she wouldn't have been able to hear them if he hadn't been so close.

He couldn't feel it? The sense of wrongness hanging all around it? "It's the kelpie."

Budge grabbed the boy by the collar and shook him. "Coward." He tossed the boy in the direction of the kelpie. The boy fell to his knees in the dirt. "Go."

The boy glanced up and shook his head.

Budge's face turned crimson. He stalked toward the boy, one fist raised in a clear threat.

Gavran grabbed her arm. "This is our chance then. I'll stop him, and you can use it as a distraction to remove the bridle."

Her legs wouldn't move. Why wouldn't her legs move? She glanced at the kelpie, and the heavy sensation in her chest slithered down into her belly.

She wiped her fingers over her eyes. It couldn't be fear stopping her. The kelpie appeared far less terrifying than the other monsters they'd faced, and she'd been able to charge straight at them. And this time they weren't even planning to fight the beast. They were going to free it. It shouldn't want to kill them for that. The danger to them was minimal.

So why couldn't she make herself move?

She peeked at the kelpie again. Bile rose up in her throat, and she choked. It was as if her body were responding to a sense of evil that her eyes couldn't see. As if that evil could run deeper because of the innocent shell it hid inside. Because the people it deceived and killed wouldn't be willingly turning themselves over to a known evil. They'd be innocent victims.

"Ceana?" Gavran's voice had taken on an urgent tone. "We're going to miss our chance."

She turned her back on the clearing and sank down. "We need

to wait. We need to talk to it first. Maybe we can wring a promise from it in exchange for freeing it. Somehow keep it from harming anyone once it's loose."

He knelt down beside her. "We already made a deal with the brollachan."

Her throat burned. She swallowed hard. "It doesn't need to know that."

The thwack of a slap hitting flesh ricocheted through the air.

Gavran flinched. "I don't understand. What changed from a moment ago?"

How could she explain it to him? Why couldn't everyone sense the deep evil flowing off of it? Or maybe Budge's son could, and that's why the boy would rather take a beating than interact with the kelpie. She reached a hand out toward Gavran. "You can't sense the evil when you look at it?"

Gavran glanced through the brush once more, then knelt down next to her, and squeezed her hand. "It's just a horse. A large horse to be sure, but not an unnatural one." He cupped her cheeks in both of his hands, turned her face up, and kissed her gently. "But I believe you. We'll wait and approach it back at the stable when we can talk to it alone."

She wrapped her arms around him and buried her face in his neck. Some of the tension spiraling through her body broke away and sloughed off. She wasn't a mistake to him. She wasn't someone who always did the wrong thing. She wasn't someone who made up wild stories. When he looked at her, he saw someone smart and capable.

Hopefully he wasn't wrong. Because if he was, she'd just made an already challenging task harder and let a boy take a beating for nothing.

CHAPTER 7

*C*eana woke with a start. Her bottom and legs were chilled and stiff, the ground underneath having lost the warmth of the day now that the sun had gone down. The left side of her body, though, was comfortable where she'd fallen asleep leaning against Gavran.

He smiled at her, his teeth strangely white in the moonlight. "We traded places tonight. You slept while I watched."

She had, hadn't she? She stretched slightly. The yard around them was empty and quiet other than the occasional snort and shuffle from the livestock and the faint muffled sounds of men talking softly to each other. She let her gaze seek the sound. Two men stood on watch at the far edge of the buildings.

"I must have finally caught up on all the rest the dreams stole from me," Gavran whispered. "And you..." He ran his fingers lightly along her hair line and over the edge of her jaw, leaving warmth in their wake. "You slept. You trusted me to stay awake."

His voice was so vulnerable, a thread of grief still trailing behind it. The betrayals that had happened in their past—intentional and unintentional—would always be there. He couldn't erase the fact that he'd accidentally fallen asleep on the night of the wishes, when she'd needed him most. She couldn't change the fact that she'd made decisions that affected both their futures without his consent.

But maybe it didn't have to define their relationship going forward. Maybe it could mould and grow them instead. They knew better now where they were each weak. And strong.

She leaned forward and caught his lips in a kiss. "I trust you above anyone else."

He slumped against her, then returned her kiss, slow and deep. Too soon, he broke away.

It was time.

"We should be able to sneak in to speak to the kelpie now." He got to his feet and helped her up. "It's been near an hour since I saw anyone other than the guards."

She brushed dirt and grass off the backside of her skirt. "Did anyone try to run us off while I slept?"

Gavran shook his head. "Anyone who asked I told we wanted to petition the master for work but that he hadn't had time to see us today. That seemed to satisfy."

They picked their way toward the stables, weaving carefully around a wagon heaped high with hay and clay mounds left behind by the masons. The ground was packed hard as cobblestones and worn free of grass beneath her feet. The part moon above gave only enough light to turn everything around them into shadowy heaps until they were almost on top of them.

Something moved in the corner of Ceana's vision. The night was breezeless. It couldn't be fabric flapping in the wind. She slowed and turned her head.

A slight figure crept along the wall of the stable, stopping, looking behind her, then starting again, the sequence repeated every few feet. Off to meet with a lover?

They couldn't afford for her to see them acting furtive any more than she seemed to want to be seen.

Ceana grabbed Gavran's elbow. He pulled up, and she

squeezed his arm before he could ask a question and give them away. She turned her gaze back to the young woman. Gavran's eyes followed her motion.

The closer the young woman got, the more her features took shape. Maybe sixteen to eighteen years. Her cloak was rough spun, but the gown peeking out from underneath moved with a fluidity that spoke of a much finer material.

The young woman crept forward another few feet. She glanced around. Ceana held her breath, even though they were too distant for breathing to give them away. Hopefully, if they held still, they'd blend into the other dark shapes around the yard.

The young woman ducked into the stables.

Gavran huffed softly. He leaned his head close to hers. "Do we wait?"

Maybe she was only meeting someone here but not planning to spend their time together in the stables. Especially if the fine clothes she seemed to want to hide said anything about who she was. Perhaps she intended to flee her dadaidh's household. With how he treated his son, no doubt his daughter fared no better.

"We get closer so we can hear when she leaves."

They moved to the side of the stable door closest to them rather than risking crossing in front of it. Gavran tapped her on the shoulder and pointed in one direction. She faced the opposite. At least if the young woman was meeting someone and he hadn't arrived yet, they'd spot him in time to hide.

"All I want is to be with you." A man's rumbling voice came from inside the stable. His tone was low enough that he had to be trying to keep from being heard, but the timbre of his voice made it so that his words carried anyway.

A finger of cold slithered its way down from the base of Ceana's scalp to her lower back. Her skin pimpled and quivered in its trail. A voice that deep should have been appealing, but there was a dark edge to it that reminded her a little of Hugh

MacDonald. And Hugh MacDonald had spent all his time plotting how to murder Lord MacDonald, Salome, and their unborn child.

Ceana moved closer to the door and strained to hear the reply.

"I'm trying. I promise." The female voice was pleading, almost desperate. "I don't know where my dadaidh's hidden the key. It's not with his others."

What could they possibly be trying to unlock? A trunk of coins? Maybe to pay for their flight from Budge?

"I can't hang on much longer." Extra gravel entered the man's voice.

"I could bring a *sgian* right now—"

"No, I've told you. It won't work."

Bile rose up in Ceana's throat. She swallowed hard against the burn. The man talking to Budge's daughter had said *no*, rather than *nay*. The same way Salome did. The same way the banshee had.

She wasn't speaking to a man at all. She was speaking to the kelpie.

Ceana's stomach twisted hard enough that she doubled over slightly. Budge's daughter sounded like she was infatuated with the kelpie. How long had it been wooing her to be able to turn her against her dadaidh?

The young woman couldn't possibly know what the kelpie was. She wouldn't be fool enough to consider setting it free if she was. *You're considering setting it free*, a tiny voice whispered in her head. *You planned to do that exact thing.*

"As soon as I'm free, we can escape together." An unnatural silkiness entered the kelpie's voice. It was so much like a caress that it almost seemed indecent to listen in. "Even once you free me from the curse, I'm sure I can hang on to this form long enough to carry you away from here."

Ceana's legs went out from under her. Gavran caught her

before she hit the ground. He kept his hands securely under her elbows and pulled her closer.

Ceana leaned heavily on him. If Budge's daughter mounted the kelpie after setting it free, she'd die. That this was part of their plan proved that she didn't know what the kelpie was. She must think him a man cursed to live in the form of a horse and carry out hard labor so long as he wore the bridle on his head. They had to warn her. And now more than before, they needed a promise from the kelpie before they freed it that would prevent it from harming people.

Gavran tugged her back away from the stable door.

The action yanked her attention to the world around her. She'd missed the end of the conversation, and now the stable had gone quiet. Footsteps approached them from inside.

Ceana had to talk to her, had to try to convince her of the folly of what she planned to do. She couldn't risk that the girl would find the key and return to free the kelpie before Ceana and Gavran could make a deal with it.

Stay hidden, she mouthed at Gavran. Hopefully he could make out her words in the dark. She had a better chance of convincing Budge's daughter of the truth if it were one woman speaking to another.

She waited until the young woman was far enough away from the stables that the kelpie wouldn't overhear—she hoped. Who knew what kind of improved hearing might come along with its other supernatural abilities.

"Please," she whispered, stepping into the young woman's path. "I need to speak with you about someone we both know." She inclined her head towards the stables.

The young woman startled and threw up her hands in a *stay back* gesture. "I don't know you, so I doubt we have any common associations." There was a haughty edge to her voice, but a strain as well, as if the tone didn't come naturally to her.

There was no point in trying to manipulate or deceive. What

the young woman needed was the truth. "I overheard your conversation in the stable."

The young woman lowered her arms and tipped her chin up. "You must be mistaken. I couldn't sleep so I came out to visit my horse. Now I'll be heading back inside."

She sidestepped but Ceana moved in front of her again.

Ceana's throat muscles tightened slightly. The girl could call for the guards at any time. Ceana stepped back, putting more room between them. Trying to show she wasn't a threat. "He's not really a horse." How could she approach this so that the girl would listen, so that she'd hear. "And I'm here to help you."

The girl took a step forward, her eyes so wide in the dark that the moonlight glinted off the whites. "You know about him? And you can help me free him?"

The hope in her voice speared straight into Ceana's chest and left a bruise that she wasn't sure would heal. Why did she have to be the one to take that hope away from her?

She knew better than most how feeling trapped wore a person down a little more each day. How some days the only thing that kept a body going was daydreaming about what it would be like to escape. What it would be like to find someone who valued you, instead of seeing only how you could benefit them.

She had escaped. She had found someone who valued her. In telling this girl the truth, she'd be taking something away from her that she might never get back—the hope of being able to do the same.

But at least she'd be alive to try.

"I'm not here to help you free him. But I am here to help you. He's a kelpie, and if you free him and ride away with him, he'll drag you underwater and leave nothing for your family to find but your liver."

The young woman cringed back. "Lies." The words came out as a hiss.

Ceana bit her bottom lip. She was a complete *eejit*. All she'd experienced in the past year had made her far too blunt with her words. This girl was so naïve and trusting that she hadn't been nearly suspicious enough about a stranger approaching her in the dark and claiming to know about kelpies.

But was there a softer way to tell someone they'd been courted by a monster? Perhaps she could have left off the part about him feeding on her, but then how would the girl have understood the risks? Gavran might have been able to find a gentler way had she not banished him to observing from the shadows. Then again, the girl might have immediately called for the guards had they both confronted her. She certainly would have had Gavran attempted to speak to her alone.

Ceana glanced back at the stables. Gavran's outline was only visible from where they stood because she knew where to look and had his size and shape engraved on her heart.

"A witch cursed him. Trapped him in the form of a horse." A quaver had entered the girl's voice. An attempt not to cry? Or a touch of anger? "He *loves* me. I don't know you from Eve. Why should I believe you over him?"

She had no proof to offer the young woman. She had to give her something. At least enough to delay her. If she and Gavran could release the kelpie before the young woman did, then they wouldn't have to worry about it riding off with her and taking her to a gruesome end.

She'd give her what she had and pray it was enough. "The bridle he's wearing is what keeps him a slave to your dadaidh. That's why he wants you to take it off. That's why your dadaidh has the key. Normal bridles don't need locks." It was a bit of a guess. The brollachan had—of course—neglected to tell them that the bridle controlling the kelpie was special and wouldn't be able to be removed with a few buckles.

The young woman crossed her arms over her chest, but the motion seemed more protective than defensive. "How do I know you're not the witch who cursed him? You might be trying to trick me to keep him under your spell."

Why was it people always seemed to think she was a witch when she told them the truth about monsters?

But the petulance in the young woman's tone suggested that her point might have hit home. "If I'd cursed him, I'd have the key to his bridle. But your dadaidh has the key."

"That still doesn't prove he's a kelpie. He could be one of my dadaidh's enemies, and my dadaidh paid you to trap him." The confrontation melted from the girl's words as she spoke until they were more a plea.

Ceana's arms ached. She wanted to tug the girl to her and hold her in a tight embrace until she understood that she didn't need someone else to give her value. But that was a lesson she couldn't give tonight. She'd have to settle for giving the girl enough years of life to learn it herself. The hard way, as Ceana had. "The reason he doesn't want you cutting the bridle off him isn't because the leather can't be cut. It's because *sgian* blades are made of iron, and a *sgian* would burn him if it touched his skin. Fae like kelpies are vulnerable to iron. It's one of the only things that can hurt them."

The young woman sucked in a sharp breath. The moon came out from behind a cloud, caught her cheeks, and made them glitter. Tears.

"I'm sorry," Ceana whispered. There wasn't much else she could say.

The young woman pointed a finger at her. "Get off my dadaidh's land. Now. Or I'll see you regret it." She spun and fled for the house.

Ceana took a running step after her, then stopped. What did she think she was going to do? Tackle her to the ground. That wouldn't stop the girl from giving their description to Budge's guards if she chose to. In fact, it'd only bring those guards down on their heads faster. If Ceana let her go, the girl might stay silent at least temporarily so she didn't have to explain why she'd left her home in the middle of the night.

Watching her go, though, was like watching her younger self run from the truths she hadn't wanted to face.

She and Gavran had to make their deal with the kelpie before Budge's daughter brought the whole of Budge's guards down upon them. If the young woman spotted them still here on the morrow, she certainly would. The kelpie would have to suffer a few iron burns because they certainly couldn't wait around anymore trying to find the key.

CHAPTER 8

*G*avran moved up beside Ceana. Her spine was straight, her shoulders back, and her head up. It made her look strong and confident. Which meant that inside she was probably feeling the opposite. The weaker she felt, the stronger she seemed to try to appear, like strapping armor over her most vulnerable parts.

He wrapped his arms around her. "The truth matters, even if hearing it hurts at the time. We wouldn't have been doing her any favors if we let her keep walking a path that could only lead to harm."

The tension came out of her slowly, as if it were liquid that had to physically drain away one raindrop-sized portion at a time.

Finally, she slumped against him and her arms threaded around his waist. "She just wants someone to love her."

Gavran ran his hand over her back. How much less heartache would there be in the world if people only believed that they had been loved from the moment of conception by the God who created them? It'd certainly prevent some of the pain that came from looking for acceptance in other places.

For most, thankfully that didn't mean trying to find it in the embrace of a demon.

He glanced up. The moon had stopped rising and was starting to descend again. "We need to speak to the kelpie. We might not have long now."

Ceana sucked in a long breath and the firmness entered her body again, like she was putting on armor.

He let her go. Maybe if they survived this final test, they could live in peace long enough that she could hang her armor up and let it rust. He'd do whatever it took to see that happen.

They crept into the stable. The darkness was deeper here, without even the stars above, and the air was thick with the hot scents of horse sweat, manure, and urine.

His eyes adjusted so slowly that he couldn't have pinpointed the moment when he went from being unable to make out any but the broadest shapes to being able to see the wooden slats of the stalls and the horses' twitching ears.

But all the horses looked the same to him. More than one was large and black. How were they supposed to know which was the kelpie? It wasn't like it'd had any clear distinguishing features. At least not any that he'd been able to see from the distance they'd been at when they saw it earlier. And that had been in full sun.

"Do you see it?" he whispered.

Ceana nodded very slowly. The movement reminded him of a rabbit trying not to be spotted by a hawk. She didn't move forward.

He squinted and tried to clear his mind, but whatever she saw or felt from the kelpie, he couldn't catch it. Was it because he'd been infected by the nuckalevee venom? Had living with unseelie poison inside him made him blind to evil? Or at least less sensitive to it? But he'd wanted to knock Budge unconscious for the way he treated his son earlier, so he could still spot evil in men.

Ceana edged forward and to the right. A tall black horse stood with its head over the stall door. It turned its gaze toward them.

Her step stuttered slightly, then she evened it out and strode forward.

So that was the kelpie.

Ceana stopped outside of where the kelpie would have been able to reach her had it snaked out its neck to bite.

He stopped next to her. Ceana's hand bumped his. Accidentally? But her fingers in that slight brush had seemed to tremble. And she wouldn't want to show any weakness to the kelpie.

No sound came from Ceana. He glanced at her. Her throat worked like she wanted to speak but couldn't make the words come out. She looked at him. Her pupils were blown wide. She gave a little shake of her head.

Perhaps she was afraid enough that she couldn't get her words to come out without a telltale tremble. Whatever was going on, her message was clear. He'd have to handle this negotiation.

He jutted his chin forward. "We're here to make a deal. We'll free you. In exchange, you must make a binding vow that you won't harm another human being for as long as you exist."

The kelpie stomped its hoof and tossed its head, sending its thick, dark mane flying. "No deal."

The voice was deep and vibrated in Gavran's bones. Its mouth hadn't moved, but he would have taken an oath that he'd heard its voice with his ears rather than only in his mind.

Had he laid their offer out too honestly? Perhaps he should have asked it first if it wanted to be freed. But then he might have come across as stupid.

Dealings with the fae made about as much sense as trying to sail a boat wrongside up. He fisted his hands, then shook them out. Wherever they ended up after this, he wouldn't bargain for so much as a chicken. He'd had enough of bargaining to last a lifetime.

For now, though, he had to answer the kelpie. Pushing it to accept their offer seemed like it would make them appear too desperate. So a question perhaps. "You think you'll receive a better offer?"

Ceana didn't give him the slightest hint as to whether he was approaching this correctly or not. She stood so unnaturally still he might have feared she was dead had she not been on her feet.

The kelpie turned its head so one dark eye stared directly at him. The eye was the same soft liquid brown of every other horse he'd looked at in the course of his life. Budge couldn't have spotted it out grazing and thought *this is a magical creature I can exploit.* So had he turned the tables on the kelpie? When it'd tempted him to ride, had he found a way to bridle it instead?

The kelpie snorted. "Your offer wasn't even tempting enough to be called by that name. Give up human hearts and kidneys and tender flesh all seasoned with salt water? What good is freedom if it means I starve."

Its voice was more refined than a lord's, the accent deceptively smooth and haughty. And calm.

A sour taste filled Gavran's mouth. No being should be able to speak of eating a human near whole in that tone of voice. "You'll starve if you stay here." He glanced meaningfully back at the wagon piled with hay resting outside the stable door. "Unless you've developed a taste for dry grass."

That slight provocation seemed like something Ceana would say, didn't it?

The kelpie lifted its upper lip in the way that normal horses sometimes did that gave them the appearance of laughter. "For a generation, perhaps. But I was here long before any of you, and I'll be here when your bones have turned to dust." It blew out a breath. "But I won't have to wait that long."

The kelpie was convinced, then, that Budge's daughter would set it free. "If you mean the girl, she knows what you are now. She won't be back."

The kelpie tossed its head, lifting its thick forelock away from its eyes. "Did she tell you about her father, the man who's keeping me here? She's told me. Half the children around here are likely his by-blows. His workers can't keep their wives to themselves if they want to keep the job that feeds them." The kelpie's gaze shifted to Ceana, then back to Gavran. "He always returns them eventually, though sometimes they've not quite as pretty as when they left."

The tone of the kelpie's voice was amused, as if hearing about Budge's abuse of the women under his authority made its servitude worth it.

Heat burned up from Gavran's middle, through his neck, and down his arms. Had Ceana not been unusually mute, she would have said it was a pity they couldn't feed Budge to the kelpie. He liked to think he'd argue with her that no one deserved that fate, but he wasn't certain he'd have been able to say the words with any conviction.

"I do wonder if that will change once he's made himself a lord off the strength of my back." The kelpie let the words dangle in the stillness. "I doubt it. If there's one thing my kind has learned from our time roaming the earth, it's that giving someone more power rarely ever brings out their best qualities."

A compulsion to find the key and tear the kelpie's bridle off immediately raced through him. The touch on his mind felt familiar, as if it were walking the paths the nuckalevee venom had already forged. He took a step closer to the kelpie.

Ceana made a strangled sound from beside him. Her hand closed around his wrist, and her nails cut into his skin.

Christ preserve him. With the quickly whispered prayer, the tugging on his mind eased, even though he could still feel the kelpie working on him. He stepped back.

Ceana dragged him from the stables. Once they were far enough away that not even a supernatural being could hear them, she bent over her knees and sucked in air. Her body shuddered.

A feeling like spiders skittering over his skin replaced the calm he'd felt. Had the calm been the kelpie working to take down his defenses from the moment they'd stepped inside the stables? Of all the monsters they'd faced, the kelpie had seemed the most benign on first appearance.

Ceana straightened. "I've never felt anything like that before. It was different from the others. The kelpie... Every time I look at it..." She shook her head as if she weren't sure how to finish her thought. "I don't think it's ever going to make a deal with us. No more than a cat would make a deal with a mouse."

Bile burned up his throat, and he swallowed hard against it. "Where does that leave us if it won't bargain?"

CEANA DREW in another deep breath, her lungs still refusing to expand enough to give her the air she needed despite being away from the kelpie. As soon as they'd stepped into the stables, the air had thickened and her brain had slowed the same way it might if a bandit held a *sgian* to her throat on the road. The evil coming from the kelpie had been deeper than she'd been able to put into words.

Gavran clearly hadn't felt it the way she had since he'd been able to attempt to negotiate with the kelpie the way they'd planned.

Her legs quivered. She wasn't going to regain her breath or her strength by pretending nothing was wrong. She sat on the hard-packed dirt.

Nothing had ever looked at her as prey before. The other unseelie they'd dealt with had all wanted something from them or had wanted to kill them, but that wasn't quite the same as coming face to face with something that wanted to feast on your insides before the life had left your eyes.

Gavran dropped to the ground beside her, as if sitting in the pathway was the most natural thing in the world. He took her hand in his.

He'd asked a question, hadn't he? He'd said something at least.

He ran his thumb over her knuckles softly. "Maybe it's time to walk away. Leave the kelpie where it is if it won't bargain. If this were a bear who'd gotten a lust for human flesh or a rabid wolf, we wouldn't even be considering setting it free."

She picked through his words slowly, her mind still sluggish. Aye, she wouldn't set free a bloodthirsty bear or a rabid wolf. But there'd be no good purpose in doing so. Even if they couldn't get the kelpie to agree to their deal, freeing it was what they'd agreed to do for the information they needed. Information that would finally set her free.

But did that mean she was sacrificing others' lives to spare her own? Could she be held responsible for what the kelpie did if they freed it? She wasn't forcing it to kill anyone. She wasn't killing anyone, but that would be the outcome of releasing the creature.

She dropped her gaze to their clasped hands, hers wrapped up so tenderly in his. These choices seemed so easy to Gavran. Right and wrong so clear.

But they weren't. At least not to her. Where he saw clear water, she saw mud and silt. And shouldn't she sometimes at least be able to choose what was best for her?

She'd been staring at their hands so long they almost stopped making sense. His fingers, her fingers, skin to skin. Like they were bound together.

But they weren't yet. Maybe he wouldn't want her once he realized how selfish her heart truly was. Was it possible he'd made up a picture of her in his head, and once he learned the truth, he would be glad they hadn't married? She knew him. She had a whole lifetime of experience knowing him. He was only beginning to know her again.

Her throat tightened, and she swallowed hard against it. Better he know now. She'd never wanted him on the basis of a lie. "We knew going in we'd have to do whatever the brollachan asked, and that whatever it asked would be bad. It's the only way to get the fairy's name. It's the only way to be free of the wishes."

"We don't have to do it." He brought her hand to his lips and pressed a kiss to its back, the touch urgent even though his lips were light. "We can go back to Duntulm Castle, wed in the chapel, and spend the rest of our lives safe within their walls."

The kiss sent shivers through her skin. She crawled into his lap, wrapped her arms around his neck, and pressed her face into his shirt until the rough fabric dug into her cheek. He'd wanted to wed as soon as he'd been cured of the nuckalevee venom. He'd wanted the intimacy that came with marriage, but he'd also wanted to make that pledge before the Almighty that he'd care for her for the rest of his life. He'd wanted to give her reassurance that he wouldn't leave her. He'd argued passionately for it. The choice to wait had been hers.

And nothing had changed. "You know we can't."

His lips pressed into her temple, into the line above her eyebrow. "We could test the edges of the curses. Maybe you'd be safe as long as we're both inside the castle walls. We could have a good life."

Her heart tugged slightly. Giving up on a cure for the cursed wishes would be the easiest, safest path if they had a plan in place to deal with the consequences. And they wouldn't have to set a kelpie back loose in the world.

So why didn't it feel like enough? Why did it feel like she'd be giving Gavran half a life? Giving herself the same. "As long as Ihon and Salome rule as lord and lady. As long as we never leave Duntulm Castle. Never mend with your family. Never find my brother. Never have bairns of our own."

Gavran flinched under her hands. Eliezer thought that perhaps the cursed wishes would break if one of them died, but he couldn't make them any promises. So if they had children and Gavran died, she might not be able to care for them. It'd been the point that had finally convinced Gavran to wait when they'd had this discussion the first time. Children would naturally come once they wed. They had to have the cure first.

He kissed her again, feather light. "Before we thought you'd be cured within a few days. We weren't gambling with death yet again. The deaths of others. Our deaths. The unseelie thrive on evil. What guarantee do we have that the kelpie won't kill us as soon as we free it? Isn't the risk of living with the cursed wishes still better than that?"

Memories flooded her of the year spent under the wishes. Of what she'd seen. Of what she'd done and been forced to do. He wouldn't say what he did if he understood the depth of it. But he couldn't. "I'd marry you if my malady was only physical. If I took fits or had a bad leg. But this is different. I need to come into married life without the taint of the wishes hanging over every-thing. I won't put that on you, or on our future bairns, or on myself. It wouldn't be fair or right, even if you agreed to it. We'd always regret it if I did and it didn't turn out the way we hoped."

He pulled back from her and stroked her hair from her face with both hands. "We'd always regret it if we did this, too. Would you ever be able to stop thinking about what the kelpie was doing free in the world?"

An aching lump built at the point where her throat met her body. Nay, she wouldn't. She'd watch their children play and only be able to think about whether the kelpie had killed someone else's son or daughter since she'd loosed it back into the world. She'd hold Gavran and every moment of closeness would be tainted by the knowledge that someone else might be grieving for the husband the kelpie took, starving because of the husband the kelpie took, unprotected because of the husband the kelpie took.

"Budge isn't a good man. A man like that shouldn't be lord on the isle. Who's to say what he'll be able to do if we leave him in control of a supernatural being?"

The protest sounded weak to her own ears. There were other, better ways to stop Budge from causing turmoil on the isle.

Assuming he was even planning to usurp the position of lord. That might have been the kelpie feeding their own suspicions, or the kelpie could have fed Budge a tale that had him believing he needed the protection of permanent walls, one that had nothing to do with him trying to horde power.

"We can tell Lord MacDonald what we've seen," Gavran said as if he'd heard her thoughts. "He'll know how to deal with Budge before things go too far."

"Stopping Budge might be considered interfering in the war between the seelie and unseelie. It could put Salome and Lord MacDonald in danger."

"Then Salome will tell Eliezer about the kelpie. The seelie court will handle it."

Perhaps.

She tried to summon up enough fire to continue the argument, but when she thought about freeing the kelpie her heart ached and when she thought about walking away there was a quiet in her spirit that made no sense given the circumstances.

Gavran pressed a kiss to her forehead. "We don't have to give up. It might seem like there's no other way right now, but we have to trust the Almighty. He parted the sea for the Israelites to walk through when they were escaping Egypt. He can make a way for us when it seems like there isn't one."

She nodded and wriggled out of his lap. "Do you think we can take the risk of staying one more day? Try again on the morrow? Maybe the kelpie will be willing to bargain once Budge's daughter doesn't return." She had to believe that the girl's tears meant she'd gotten through to her. She'd done that much at least. Protected that one life.

Gavran nodded slowly. "We'll have to stay hidden. I'm certain she was telling truth about sending the guards after you if she sees you again."

CEANA JERKED UPRIGHT, her mind muzzy enough from lack of sleep that she wasn't entirely sure if she was still awake or dreaming. The night wasn't as dark, but dawn hadn't arrived yet.

Gavran's arm dropped from where he must have had it draped across her, and he grunted. "What's wrong?"

She rubbed her gritty eyes. Shouts echoed from the center of Budge's settlement.

She scrambled to her feet. Were they under some sort of attack? Maybe that's why Budge had been building defenses. Maybe they were far enough away from Duntulm Castle that bandits were a threat.

A woman's scream struck through the night, and a man sprinted toward Ceana carrying a torch. She jumped backwards. He brushed so closely by her that he would have run her down had she not moved.

Gavran joined her. His hair stuck up on one side and grass interwove with it. He glanced after the man. "What's—"

He sucked in a gasp.

Ceana spun in the direction he was staring.

In the center of the buildings, in front of the stable, a huge black horse reared up, its legs striking the air. The small group of men who'd already reached the scene leaped out of the way. The man with the torch joined them, lighting the situation.

The horse reared up again. A slight figure clung to its back.

Ceana's mouth went dry. It wasn't a horse. It was the kelpie. And the figure on its back could only be Budge's daughter.

CHAPTER 9

$\mathcal{C}$ eana sprinted forward, Gavran right behind her.

How had this happened? She'd warned the girl. She'd seemed to believe her. That couldn't have been more than a few hours earlier.

The kelpie lashed out with its hind legs, keeping the men who'd surrounded it from getting too close. Ceana skidded to a stop.

Gavran grabbed her arm and pulled her back an extra step. "Its bridle is gone."

He was right. The kelpie's large head was bare, no sign of the bridle Budge had used to capture it in sight.

The man with the torch raised it aloft, as if he were hoping the sight of the fire would send the kelpie back into the stables where they'd be able to block it in.

The flickering light illuminated a seeping wound along the kelpie's cheek.

Ceana sucked in a breath. The girl had gone for a *sgian*, despite the kelpie insisting she find the key instead. "It's my fault."

Gavran kept his eyes on the kelpie. "What are you talking about?"

"I told her the kelpie was lying when it said she wouldn't be able to cut the bridle off because it was magical. I was trying to prove to her what it was."

Instead, the girl had used that information to free a monster.

Ceana's stomach twisted. She never should have told her that. Why hadn't she considered that the girl might use the new knowledge to free the kelpie instead? She'd spent weeks, if not months, speaking to it. She'd believed its stories and professions of love enough that she'd been willing to sneak around her dadaidh's private rooms to look for the key, risking his wrath if she were caught. Of course she wouldn't give up her trust in the kelpie on the word of a stranger, no matter how good an argument that person made.

"Jump down, Annabel!" A familiar voice yelled. "I'll catch you."

Ceana turned. Budge stood as close to the kelpie as he could safely get, his arms upraised.

"I can't." The girl's voice was high-pitched and nearly hysterical. "I can't let go."

The kelpie reared again, higher than before, nearly vertical, as if to show off the truth of her words. The girl—Annabel—threw her hands out to the side, not holding on to anything, and her back arched. Her legs and bottom stayed firmly connected to the kelpie.

The kelpie came back to all fours, and the girl snapped forward again. There was nothing natural about the way she'd kept her seat. Gavran swore quietly beside her.

Annabel was trapped. She wasn't going to be able to free herself.

One man had a rope out now, as if he still thought Annabel was somehow just too afraid to leap off the plunging beast. It wouldn't work. Without the bridle, the kelpie would snap anything they tried to use to recapture him. Or at least so the stories said.

Ceana clutched Gavran's arm. "See if you can find the bridle. Maybe it can be mended."

Gavran tossed her a look that said he felt there were about as much chance of that as a moneylender forgiving a debt. He ran for the stables anyway.

Though whether or not the kind of patch they'd have time for now would work was another matter. Budge must have had a bridle worked with iron wires woven within. It was the only thing that made sense for how the bridle controlled the kelpie. There had to be places where Annabel had been able to cut through the leather, places where the wire didn't run, or she couldn't have removed it. So maybe that meant they'd be able to tie it on. Unless of course she'd found the key after all. In that case, they wouldn't be able to do anything without the key itself.

But to get the bridle back on, they'd have to get close to the kelpie. It'd never allow it. It was free and had a fresh meal on its back. However Budge had fooled it the first time, it clearly wasn't stupid enough to be taken in again. And in the few minutes she'd been watching, it'd managed to move closer to the outskirts of the ring of buildings and freedom.

Ceana shoved forward, past the men, toward Budge. "You need to kill it."

Budge didn't so much as glance in her direction. Had he even heard her over all the other noise?

"Master Budge!" She yelled the words. "You need to kill it."

Budge pivoted in her direction. His expression was darker than the sky during a thunderstorm. "Go back to the kitchen where you belong, girl. We don't need you getting underfoot."

He turned to the kelpie and his daughter.

A strange heat like boiling water overflowing a pot bubbled up inside her. She wouldn't allow him to sacrifice his daughter on his own pride. She and Gavran wouldn't be in their current position if her own dadaidh had been the man he should have been.

She grabbed Budge's tunic and yanked. He took an unsteady step back and whirled on her.

Memories of all the men who'd taken their anger out on her flashed through her mind, and it screamed at her to move away. She planted her feet instead. "You know what it is and what it'll do if it escapes with her."

The snarl fell from Budge's lips.

On the opposite side of the kelpie and the ring of men trying to toss a rope over it, Gavran emerged from the stable. He led a saddled and bridled horse, as if he'd read her thoughts before she'd even had them about what would need to be done if the kelpie fled.

He glanced in her direction and held up a *sgian* and the lengths of leather that must have been the kelpie's bridle. Budge's daughter hadn't just sliced it from the kelpie's head. She'd cut it to pieces. Though whether that idea had been hers or the kelpie's, they might never know.

Budge reached for Ceana as if he wanted to shake her for her words.

She slipped out of his reach. "It's going to break free. Your men need to already be mounted up when that happens. They won't be able to catch it otherwise. Your only chance is to arm them with iron and kill it before it can reach water deep enough to submerge."

Budge made a sputtering noise. "Are you mad, woman? That creature's the path to a better life for my family."

All the things she would have liked to say to her own dadaidh burned the back of her tongue. She swallowed them down. Budge wasn't her dadaidh. Maybe he could still be made to see sense. "At the cost of your daughter?"

An expression she couldn't untangle flashed across Budge's face. He shot a look at the kelpie and his daughter, then back at her.

"Athol!" His voice ricocheted over the other sounds. "Clyde!

Saddle horses and gather spears."

The man holding the torch passed it off to one of the others and ran for the stables. The kelpie kicked out and clipped him in the side. The man flew sideways with a cry. He hit the ground hard and lay there. A moan keened out.

Two men split away from corralling the kelpie and sprinted toward the fallen man.

Nay. Nay. There wouldn't be enough to hold the kelpie.

"Go back." She screamed the words, but the men didn't seem to hear her.

Budge's gaze locked on her. He yelled for the men to return as well.

They glanced at him as if unsure of his orders.

The kelpie swung its head in Ceana and Budge's direction. For a moment, its eyes seemed to glow, and something about the tilt of its head made her think it was smiling inside.

"I win," the kelpie's supernatural voice invaded her mind. "I told you I would."

It burst forward toward the gap the three missing men had left. A burly man leapt in its path, waving his arms the way he would to turn a normal horse from its path. The kelpie ran him down. The man didn't move or let out a sound.

Ceana bit back a curse and turned it into a prayer instead. It would take a miracle to save Budge's daughter now. Budge's men weren't mounted or armed. They'd never be able to catch the kelpie in time.

SWEAT POPPED out on Gavran's upper lip. The kelpie's tail streamed out behind it as it fled. Budge screamed at his men about horses and weapons.

But he was the only one who already had them. The Almighty certainly had a way of making a man trust him and face his fears.

Apparently, he was going to be thrown onto horses until he learned his lesson.

"Ceana," he called her name. He'd lost sight of her in the chaos.

Going after Budge's daughter and the kelpie wasn't even a question. The decision to be the kind of man who could go to bed each night and wake up each morning without regrets had been made weeks ago. But he had to find Ceana first. The kelpie's chase would certainly take him outside the range of the cursed wishes, with no way to find her if he survived it.

"Here." She came up from behind him. "I'm here. We have to—"

"Aye. I know."

He boosted her onto the back of the horse and swung up after her. His feet slid into the stirrups, and she urged the horse forward. They cantered out of the yard, men scattering out of their way as they went.

The wind whipped Ceana's hair from its ties, and the strands bit his cheeks. He didn't release his grip on Ceana's waist to try to move them away. The horse's gait smoothed out as it stretched out into a run, chasing after the kelpie, but anything faster than a walk made his limbs feel like they'd melted. Good thing Ceana was the one in control. He might not have had the courage to push their horse as fast as it needed to go.

He touched the *sgian* he'd shoved into his belt. His stomach lurched in a way that had nothing to do with the horse's movement.

The *sgian* wasn't long enough to reach the kelpie from the back of their own mount.

"Is the loch closer than the seaside?" Ceana shifted her head slightly, as if she were afraid the wind would tear her words away otherwise. "We won't catch him chasing after his trail of dust. We need to guess."

Gavran closed his eyes and brought what he knew of the land

into his mind. They'd passed the loch on the way here from Duntulm. Did that place it closer than if the kelpie headed for the sea? It should. But not by much. The kelpie's decision would hinge on how threatened it felt by pursuit.

It'd been held by Budge long enough for the brollachan to hear of it. It wouldn't risk going back to that kind of captivity.

"The loch." The kelpie had gone straight, choosing the open moors, and not risking trees blocking its way to the loch. But that meant it would have to double back slightly. If they could find a path straight through the woodland Budge had been clearing, they could catch up with it. "Take the path to the clearing where we first saw it."

Ceana nodded and wheeled the horse sharply to the right. Gavran's weight shifted, and his heart tried to fly out of his mouth. Ceana threw her body in the opposite direction to balance them out.

He tightened his grip on her waist. The hilt of the *sgian* pressed into his elbow.

It hadn't lengthened. No amount of wishing could turn it into a spear or a lochabar that would let them attack the kelpie from a distance. And attacking it was the only way they were going to be able to convince it to let Budge's daughter go. They certainly didn't have time to reason with it, and bargaining hadn't worked even when there had been time.

If they caught the kelpie, one of them was going to have to leap into its back.

A sick heat flooded his face. Not one of them. It'd have to be him. Because if the kelpie managed to get too far away from him, Ceana would have no chance of stopping it. It'd carry both her and Budge's daughter underwater and have a double feast.

Should the kelpie somehow distance itself from Ceana, he'd have the wishes ensuring his success. He pushed the question of how he'd find Ceana again after from his mind. One problem at a time was plenty.

"Duck," Ceana called.

Gavran leaned down, and a branch that would have knocked him flat swept close enough to tug his clothes. He straightened and caught a flash of the moon through the trees ahead.

They were almost to the end of the wooded path. Budge had cleared it, just as they'd hoped. Lord willing, they'd come out even with or ahead of the kelpie. As long as they'd wagered true. Had it taken the road to the sea...

He wouldn't think it. He'd hold onto hope.

And though it hadn't been what they'd wanted, once they saved Budge's daughter, the kelpie would be free. They could return to the brollachan with a clear conscience and receive the fairy's name.

They burst from the treeline. In the distance, moonlight glittered off the loch like teeth, sharp and ready to swallow Budge's daughter down.

He glanced around. A black form streamed toward them, mane and tail nearly horizontal with its speed. It was headed on a collision course with them. It either hadn't spotted them or didn't believe they could stop it.

"We only have a *sgian*. I'm going to have to jump onto its back." The words tried to stick in his throat, but he forced them off his tongue. "It's the only way."

One of Ceana's hands found his. "Hand me the *sgian* and take the reins. I'll do it."

Worn leather touched his palm. She must have loosened her hold on the reins to try to pass them to him.

The urge to hold her close and tell her how much he loved her swamped him. He'd always been better at climbing trees and leaping from branch to branch when they were children. He was the stronger one and better able to drive the *sgian* deep enough into the kelpie's side to convince it to release him and Budge's daughter. The only reason for Ceana to offer to take his place was because she knew that jumping from a normal horse to another supernatural one was something straight out of his nightmares.

The kelpie was nearly close enough now. It glanced at them sidelong, but it couldn't veer away from them without also veering away from the loch.

Gavran pressed the reins back toward her. His stomach turned, and he swallowed down hot bile. He had to do this. "I'll be the one."

"Don't be an *eejit*. If you fail, I can't watch it carry you to your death." Her voice shook in a way that made it clear that she wasn't doubting him. She'd simply rather be the one who died first.

"No more than I could you. Stop arguing or I'll lose my nerve."

He released his feet from the stirrups. They flapped against the horse's sides and seemed to give it an extra burst of speed. He'd have to pull his feet under him and leap before he lost his balance. The timing would have to be perfect.

Ceana angled the horse close. So close that one more step would bring them both to the ground and likely kill them all from broken necks. "I love you."

The words sounded a little too much like a last goodbye. Maybe they would be. "And I you."

He coiled himself up and leaped.

CHAPTER 10

avran's stomach slammed into the kelpie's spine. The air shot from his lungs, and he scrabbled with his hands for anything to hold onto. They slipped over the kelpie's side, the hair slick with sweat beneath his fingers. The ground bobbed and jerked below him.

His vision blurred, then cleared.

He lay across the kelpie's back like a sack of wet grain. His palms rested against the kelpie's ribs and his legs still swayed sickeningly on the creature's opposite side, but he wasn't sliding around. The creature's magic held him—though not in the position he would have chosen. Every hard jostle threatened to force the remains of last night's meal from his stomach.

"Why are you doing this?" Budge's daughter half mumbled, half cried the words. "Why are you doing this?"

He opened his mouth to reply that he'd come to help her, but stopped the words before they left his mouth. Her words carried the exhausted tone of someone who'd been saying the same thing for so long that they didn't even realize they were speaking anymore. Like a woman pleading with the betrothed who wanted to call off their wedding.

Budge's daughter wasn't talking to him. She was speaking to the kelpie.

And clearly, now that the monster had what it wanted from her, it had stopped answering her pleas.

He wanted to drive the *sgian* between the beast's rib and dig it deep enough to hit a vital organ. No doubt that showed he was far from being like Christ, since the Lord had cried out for the forgiveness of those who'd murdered him. But it felt like a deeper cruelty that the kelpie refused to even answer her now that it'd gotten its freedom. A deeper cruelty that it'd broken her heart instead of merely eating it.

Gavran pulled his arm back to yank the *sgian* from his belt. His arm froze extended out from his side as if he pushed against a wall that wasn't there.

Christ preserve him. The monster must have interpreted his movements as an attempt to drop to the ground. The kelpie's magic wouldn't allow him to leave its back. Or to do anything that seemed like he might be trying to. He wouldn't be able to reach behind him to grab the *sgian*.

The pounding of Ceana's mount still kept pace with them, though they seemed less stable now. The horse's labored snorts spoke to its exhaustion. It might not even be able to keep pace with them to the loch. And that couldn't be far now.

His heart slammed harder against his chest than the kelpie's spine did against his stomach. There was nothing Ceana could do to help him. Even if she rammed her mount into the kelpie, it'd only injure her and her horse. The kelpie might not even feel it.

The kelpie might have a bigger feast than it bargained for after all. His plan to force the kelpie to stop had failed.

Budge's daughter's calls to the kelpie increased in volume as if she saw the loch coming and knew her fate. As if she were still hoping she'd been right about his love for her or that he'd change his mind.

She was the only one who might be able to reach the *sgian*.

What had Budge called her? Annabel. That was it. "Annabel, help me."

She looked back over her shoulder. Her face was blotchy, her eyes swollen. "I can't. He won't let me free."

Her gaze wasn't quite focused. Had her mind snapped from the trauma of what had happened? Not everyone had Ceana's iron spirit. But Ceana had been tempered long before the cursed wishes forced her to face monster after monster.

"I have the *sgian* you used on its bridle. Grab it from my waist. We can make him let us go."

Annabel shuddered, her arm bumping into him. "The smell when the iron touched him... when I cut off the bridle..." She covered her mouth as if she might vomit.

Gavran glanced at where Ceana's horse had been a moment before. They'd fallen behind, her mount's head now barely even with the kelpie's tail.

Her mouth moved. Hurry? She pointed ahead.

They must be almost to the loch.

"Annabel, look at me." Hopefully using her name would make her focus on him.

She swiveled her head around again.

"Get the *sgian* from my belt." He tried to put force—command —into his words. They didn't have time for softness and agreement.

Annabel's gaze wandered across his body, and she frowned as if noticing for the first time that he wasn't sitting astride. "He's the monster that woman warned me he was, isn't he?"

Gavran prayed wordlessly. His heart beat so hard it was a miracle it hadn't broken his ribs. She was taking too long. "Aye. Give me the *sgian*. We can stop him."

Hopefully it wasn't a lie. As soon as it touched the water, it wasn't likely to stop no matter what they did. It would know it could drown them before they could do any lasting harm to it. Perhaps eating them would even help it heal whatever wounds they'd be able to inflict. This couldn't be the first time someone had tried to fight their way free.

Something he probably should have thought about before throwing himself onto the back of a known killer.

Annabel reached back and laid her fingers on the hilt of the *sgian*. She drew it from his belt with an agonizing slowness.

He held out his hand.

Annabel's eyes went dark, as if her pupils had suddenly dilated.

Gavran sucked in a breath. Was she going to stab him instead? A last attempt to protect the kelpie. Perhaps she'd rather die with him than betray the kelpie the way it'd betrayed her.

Annabel switched the *sgian* to her right hand. Gavran tried to shift his position and couldn't. What was she doing?

The kelpie's magic held him in place. If Annabel was going to stab him in the back, there was nothing he could do about it. Maybe it would be better than being alive for whatever the kelpie did to his victims. After all, they couldn't be sure he drowned them before beginning to eat them.

From the corner of his eye, he caught movement. Annabel raising her arm? A sound from behind him that could have been Ceana screaming.

A flash of motion, and the kelpie stumbled.

Drops of something hot and sticky spattered Gavran's face.

Annabel moved again.

This time the kelpie screamed. An unearthly wail, high-pitched and feral. The hair on Gavran's arms and the back of his neck lifted.

Then he was rolling sideways through the air.

GAVRAN'S BODY crashed to the ground directly in front of her, and Ceana wrenched her horse's head to the left. The horse reacted sluggishly. They were too close. She braced for the sound and feel of hooves hitting flesh.

Nothing. She opened her eyes, though she couldn't pinpoint when she'd closed them. She pulled the horse to a stop. It didn't hesitate. Its head drooped immediately, sucking in large snorts of air. She slid from its back. Sweat and lather from the exhausted animal dampened her palms. She dropped the reins. It wasn't likely to go anywhere unless someone forced it to.

She spun back in the direction of Gavran and the kelpie. He was on his hands and knees as if he'd rolled to the side almost as soon as he touched the ground. The breath left her lungs in a rush. His quick reaction was probably what had saved him from being run over by her mount.

But where had the kelpie gone? Its fleeing form wasn't still headed for the loch. They were so close. Had the kelpie managed to drag Annabel down after everything they'd done?

She hurried to Gavran's side. The oranges and pinks of dawn were streaking the sky and gave her a clear look at him. Blood spattered his face.

Had he cracked his skull on a rock in his fall? She dropped down next to him. "Are you hurt?"

He pointed toward the water. "Stop her." His words came out forced as if the fall had knocked the wind from him and he'd only barely gotten his air back enough to speak.

She shifted her gaze to where he pointed. No more than the height of two men from the water lay the large form of the kelpie. Its legs were curled under it as if it were preparing to rest in the sun, but its head whipped back and forth like a snake trying to strike. Annabel's slim form dodged its attacks. Her arm was raised, the *sgian* clutched in her fist.

Her dress and hair were drenched with blood.

Almighty spare her. Why wasn't the *eejit* girl running? The kelpie had released her. She should be trying to flee.

Unless... Unless that blood wasn't hers.

"Hurry." Gavran's voice still sounded slightly dazed. He tried to rise to his feet but slumped back to the ground again. "She's free. It's free. We can have both."

Ceana spun around. Both. When the kelpie had Annabel and had been ready to eat her, Ceana hadn't even thought about the consequences of telling Budge he needed to kill the monster. It'd seemed like the only way. But now all she had to do to fulfill the brollachan's request was to keep the kelpie alive. She didn't have to free it. Annabel had done that. And there was no way they could force even an injured kelpie back into captivity. Not with the magical bridle in tatters.

But fulfilling the task she'd been given now meant stopping Annabel. Because if the kelpie died, the brollachan might do more than refuse to give them the fairy's name. It might kill them.

Ceana sprinted forward as Annabel lunged for the kelpie again.

The kelpie grabbed Annabel's arm in its teeth, and a sound like a branch snapping from a tree rent the air. Annabel wailed. The *sgian* fell from her grip. The kelpie whipped its head to the left dragging Annabel's body with it.

Ceana pressed herself faster. Her mouth went dry, though she couldn't be sure whether it was from fear or from trying to get enough air to keep going. She'd thought to stop Annabel from killing the kelpie, but now it seemed like she'd have to rescue the young woman rather than the other way around.

She glanced to the side. There weren't even any trees close enough for her to find a weapon that she could use without further injuring the kelpie.

The thunder of hoofbeats came from behind her. Far more than could have been made by her single, worn-out horse. She looked back.

At least five mounted men streamed toward her. Budge and his men had arrived.

Had she and Gavran waited for them, the kelpie would have dragged Annabel down into the water before Budge could have caught up with them.

They parted around her but didn't slow. A clod of dirt kicked up from one of the horse's hooves and caught her in the face. Her eyes watered, the world blurred, and she stumbled.

Another scream tore through the air, higher pitched than anything a human could make.

She scrubbed at her eyes and blinked hard. Her vision cleared, and a spiralling sensation hit her.

Budge's men were off their horses. Two stabbed at the kelpie with spears and another with a lochabar ax. A fourth man writhed on the ground, clutching at his side. Budge stood off to one side, his daughter cradled in his arms as if she were a child. From the way she slumped against him, she might be unconscious.

The kelpie wasn't moving.

Even if she ran into their midst screaming for them to stop, it'd be too late.

The kelpie was dead.

Her chance to be free of the cursed wishes died with it. But one less monster lived in the world. Her mind couldn't quite make sense of the dichotomy.

Gavran limped to her side, a hand pressed to his stomach. He wrapped his other arm around her waist. "Do you think the brollachan will give us the fairy's name? The kelpie was freed. We can argue we fulfilled our side of the bargain."

She shook her head. The fae loved loopholes and details, saying things that could be taken two ways, letting you believe one while meaning the other that was beneficial to them. Had it been true that they'd freed the kelpie and then Budge's men hunted it down and killed it without their involvement, they might have been able to still coerce the brollachan's cooperation. It might have even respected them a little for it.

There was only one problem. "We didn't free it. Annabel did."

Had they rescued the kelpie from Annabel's attack afterward, that could have counted as freeing it as well. But they hadn't even managed to do that.

Gavran kissed the top of her head. "Think of it this way, we're better off than before. We're not leaving the kelpie in Budge's hands. Lord and Lady MacDonald won't need to take a risk in reporting it to the seelie court."

She leaned into him, and her chest went tight. How was it possible that she loved him even more than she had before the fairy cursed them? Shouldn't she have loved him less with all his weaknesses and failures on display? Though, perhaps that was actually what had grown her love. She'd thought him perfect before. Now she saw an imperfect man striving to be better — strengths like his optimism standing side by side with his fears and failings.

A man she could continue to grow beside for the rest of their lives if only they could break the wishes.

Something he'd said itched at her mind. Had the kelpie not died, they'd have had to tell Salome and Lord MacDonald about it, and Salome would have had to report it to Eliezer, who could have told the court. Because fae weren't all-knowing. Only the Almighty was omniscient. The fae were more powerful than humans in some ways, but they still had to learn things.

She slipped out of Gavran's hold and grabbed his hand. "I think you're partly right. We don't have to tell the brollachan anything other than that the kelpie was freed. It might still work. We just have to get there before it finds out the truth."

CHAPTER 11

The brollachan's cottage looked as dark and uninhabited as the first time they'd approached. No smoke rose from the chimney. No wood was stacked alongside the building. No laundry hung from the branches of the nearby trees.

The skin on the back of Ceana's neck prickled. Had the brollachan moved on, hoping to cheat them from their bargain that way? They couldn't collect if they couldn't find it. Or was it waiting somewhere to ambush them?

"Do you notice how quiet it is here?" Gavran whispered. "It's like even the birds and the bugs sense the evil and avoid this place."

Ceana paused and listened. He was right. The chirps and twitters and buzz that accompanied a person anywhere else on the isle were absent here. The grove where the nuckalevee appeared each night had been the same. Like other creatures sensed the presence of a predator and stayed away.

Heaviness drew her shoulders down. The brollachan was a predator of sorts, and they were walking right up to it and waving a blood-covered cloth in front of it, hoping it'd lost its sense of smell.

"I just want this to be over." The words slipped out before she could stop them. Now wasn't the time, but they pressed against her lips like water building up behind a beaver's dam. "I'm so tired."

Gavran took her hand, lifted it to his lips, and kissed her knuckles.

She gave him her best smile and shoved her exhaustion to the back of her mind. What else could either of them do? If they'd gotten here before news of the kelpie's demise, maybe this would be the last monster they'd have to face. She clutched the idea close to her heart.

They moved slowly up to the door, and Gavran knocked.

They were knocking on the door of a demon as if they were visiting a neighbor. A hysterical giggle worked its way up Ceana's throat. She swallowed it down.

The brollachan didn't answer, but a faint shuffle-scrape seemed to come from inside.

Ceana strained her ears. Was that...? Aye, something moved within the cottage. But what reason could the brollachan have for not answering their knock?

Every moment they hesitated was another that the brollachan might learn of the kelpie's death. If the brollachan were in there, they couldn't wait for it to decide to talk to them.

Ceana touched her fingertips to the door and pushed gently. It swung open. The interior was lit only by the tiny slivers of light coming in through the high, narrow windows. They cast lines of muted glow, dust motes swirling in their path.

Gavran jerked slightly and pointed a finger with his hand kept low at his waist.

The brollachan, Caillic, whatever it chose to call itself, stood beside the table. The meat and entrails of some animal lay spread out upon it, the beefy stench of old blood and stomach offal pungent in the air. The brollachan sliced a piece of flesh from the hide, slid it into its mouth, chewed, then swiveled its head in their direction. It bared its teeth, stained red from blood.

Bile rose up in Ceana's throat. If they'd needed any further reminder of what truly controlled Caillic's body, there it was. If the creature didn't want to be so obvious about it, it could have at least roasted the meat first.

The brollachan twirled the *sgian* around in its fingers. "I didn't take you for fools, yet here you stand."

A shiver ran over Ceana's skin. It already knew what had happened. They hadn't been fast enough.

Gavran tensed beside her.

The brollachan picked up its victim's liver and bit down with a squelching noise. It chewed slowly, as if savoring the taste. "Are you going to explain your presence or merely continue to stand there tempting me?"

Ceana forced her gaze away from the mess on the table. They were here. She had to at least try. "We came for the fulfillment of your side of our bargain. The kelpie was freed."

The brollachan's lips pulled back. It threw the *sgian*. Ceana and Gavran dodged in opposite directions. The knife embedded itself in the door frame.

Ceana's heart beat an uneven rhythm in her chest as if trying to remind her that anyone with half the sense they were born with would flee. But what life would she be fleeing to? None at all. Any sort of future with Gavran, any sort of good life for her brother, depended on getting that fairy's name. The brollachan didn't understand her at all if it thought a threat so mild would chase her away.

She straightened and met the brollachan's gaze. "The kelpie is no longer enslaved. What is the name of the fairy who placed the cursed wishes on us?"

The brollachan leaned forward over the table, its nails scoring into the wood and leaving faint lines behind. "You were to free him as recompense for the death of the nuckalevee. What makes you think I will give you anything when you killed him instead?"

"We didn't—"

The brollachan snarled, an expression that shouldn't have been possible on a human face. "Because you did not drive the knife in yourself? Yes, I know the details of his death. My brethren were watching and were here before his blood turned cold." The brollachan made a *be gone* gesture with its hand. "You are fortunate I like this body and don't want to see it damaged. Leave before I change my mind."

The brollachan returned its attention to fileting the meat on the table.

Gavran tugged gently on Ceana's arm.

Ceana's shoulder muscles tensed so tightly that tingles traced their way down her arms and into her hands. Was that to be it then? They were supposed to walk away and feel grateful. Because what? Because another monster hadn't chosen to torment them?

It might not have attacked them physically, but living under the cursed wishes was torment. Fearing every moment that she might be separated from Gavran, unable to find him again, his memory of her fading as quickly as her hope. She'd go mad if she had to face that again.

So they'd have to find another way to discover the name of the fairy who cursed them. Which might mean fighting another monster or making an even worse deal with a demon like the brollachan. Placing Gavran in danger.

Nay. No more.

Somehow the brollachan was going to tell them the name. If she had to battle a monster for the identity of the fairy, it might as well be this one as any other. Perhaps if they returned with swords? Or was the brollachan immune to the fae weakness to iron thanks to inhabiting Caillic's body? It had been using a *sgian*, even eating from it without any ill effects. So iron weapons might harm Caillic, but might not touch the brollachan inside. That might work since the brollachan didn't want Caillic's body harmed. But she'd have to harm Caillic to test the theory.

They had to find another way to force it out. What would make the brollachan leave Caillic other than iron? She stomped out into the yard fast enough that Gavran let go of her.

The sunlight hit her hot and heavy, nearly blistering her skin after the damp and darkness of the brollachan's home. It was almost as if the creature had never lit a fire, and without the warmth, the dankness of the frequent Skye rains never burned away.

A hard beat rocked her chest, and she sucked in a breath. Maybe that was it. She grabbed Gavran's hand and hauled him down the road, far enough away to be sure the brollachan wouldn't overhear. They couldn't guarantee that another super-natural creature wasn't listening in, but it was better than standing right outside the brollachan's door when she gave voice to her suspicion.

She stopped. Gavran raised his eyebrows.

She squeezed his hand. "Why is it, do you think, that the brol-lachan eats its meals raw? And never seems to have a fire?"

Gavran's eyebrows came down into a V over his nose. "That's not what I was thinking you were about to say." His voice carried a hesitant note.

He knew her well enough to know something he wouldn't like was coming.

She released him and gathered up a twig, then another. She needed to move fast in case something was listening or watching. "Didn't the parish priest at least one Sunday a month preach about the fires in hell that never go out?"

"Aye." Gavran's tone turned even more cautious as he studied each movement she made. "Do I need to be worried?"

Most likely. She might be out of her head for thinking this was a good idea. She was out of her head. This was a terrible idea.

But neither Salome nor Eliezer had known any other creature than the brollachan who might be able to give them the fairy's name. It was either this plan or they had to admit defeat and live with the cursed wishes for the rest of their days.

She glanced around. She still needed some tinder to catch and hold the spark long enough for it to feed on the twigs.

An abandoned bird nest hung dilapidated from a nearby tree. She jumped and pulled part of it away, laid it on the ground, and piled her twigs on top. "I think the brollachan doesn't light fires because its afraid of them." She held out a hand toward him. "Let me have the firesteel."

Gavran waved her away and knelt down by the pile she'd made. He pulled out the firesteel and his *sgian*. "Tell me if I'm following the path you've beaten. You're going to make a torch and threaten the brollachan with it? To force it to give us the fairy's name?"

She flinched but nodded. It did sound a mite bit mad to try to force a supernatural creature to do anything. But if she were right, the fear of being touched with the fire should be enough. "It felt we failed on our first deal. I'm going to make it a new deal. It gives us the name, and I don't burn it to ashes."

One of the sparks from the firesteel leapt into the bird's nest and caught. Gavran leaned close and blew gently. "It's never going to believe you."

Never going to... Oh. If she did burn the brollachan, she'd be burning Caillic as well. She'd have to pray that the brollachan wouldn't call her bluff. Or maybe Caillic, if she could still speak for herself, would gladly suffer a burn to be free of the brollachan? Maybe, despite what the priest had said, she regretted her decision to welcome the brollachan in.

Maybe.

She tore a strip off her leine using Gavran's *sgian* and tied it around a long, thick branch. This had to end. These kinds of decisions were too much day after day. After this was over, all she wanted to have to decide was which material would be sturdiest for new clothes for Gavran and Colin, once they found him. Or which beach would be best to hunt for cockles. And whether the water was too cold to wade out into.

She dipped the tip of her makeshift torch into the small fire Gavran was stoking. The hem of her leine had been slightly damp from the grass. It smouldered, then finally caught. Keeping it from going out prematurely might take an act of the Almighty, though.

Torch in hand, she headed back to Caillic's cottage, Gavran beside her.

"Are you sure about this?" he asked. "We're about to make an enemy of a demon."

The brollachan already hated them. But it hadn't been willing to risk Caillic to punish them for their crimes. Hopefully, that would remain true after what she was about to do.

Either way, she wasn't turning back from this. "It has to end." She waved a hand at him, at the way he was still limping from his fall off the back of the kelpie. "We both know it."

Gavran nodded. His lips parted as if he wanted to say something more, but he pressed them shut and nodded again.

The fight was going out of him. He'd always been the one to check her when she pushed too far, even before the cursed wishes. The constantly battling—it was like it'd worn down his will. If for no other reason than that, she needed to end this. If she didn't, one day soon he'd go along with whatever she suggested, whether it was sane or not, whether it was moral or not. And then he wouldn't be the man she'd fallen in love with. They'd have lost the balance that made them such a good match.

She didn't stop to knock on Caillic's door. She shoved it open with her foot and entered torch first.

The brollachan hissed and backed up, abandoning its meal. "Get out."

Ceana stepped farther into the room. Gavran stopped in the

doorway behind her, his form blocking some of the sunlight, and also blocking what would be the brollachan's only route of escape should it try to flee once it realized what was about to happen. Gavran unsheathed his *sgian*.

"Give me the name of the fairy who placed the cursed wishes on us." She took another stride toward the brollachan. Hopefully it would be too busy focusing on the flame to see how much her hands shook. She pointed with her free hand towards a bucket of water in one corner. "And I'll put this out. We'll leave you in peace and never come near your home again."

The brollachan's gaze shifted a fraction between the flames and Ceana's face. "You would have to hurt the body I wear to hurt me. What would that make you?"

Ceana stared at the fire, it's yellow edges sharp like teeth. Gavran had said the brollachan wouldn't believe her, wouldn't believe that she would burn Caillic to force it to agree. Perhaps she wouldn't. But Caillic wasn't the only thing here that would burn.

She moved to the side and held the torch close enough to the wall that it started to smoke. "We killed the nuckalevee. We killed the kelpie." Not entirely true, but close enough. "You would make three. That seems fair. One for each of the wishes I've had to suffer under. Or you can give me the information I seek."

The brollachan's eyes narrowed, and the edges of her mouth hardened.

Fine then. Ceana touched the torch to the wall. The dry material caught, and flames licked up the wall. Tendrils of acrid smoke spiralled into the air.

"What are you doing?" A woman's voice. It quavered.

Ceana spun away from the wall and held up the torch. There wasn't anyone in the cottage other than her, Gavran, and the brollachan. The building had only the one room. Her torch drove out the shadows. There wasn't anywhere another woman could hide. Where had the voice come from?

Gavran still stood in the doorway, but his mouth hung open slightly. He stared at the brollachan.

The brollachan held out its hands toward her in a pleading gesture. "Please stop. My home."

Almighty spare them. That was Caillic's voice, freed from the brollachan's control. Ceana could hear the similarity now. The brollachan's tone had been more forced and pitched slightly lower, as if it hadn't been completely comfortable speaking. But the disparity was more like the voice of age compared to the voice of youth rather than a different speaker.

Caillic lunged for the water bucket. Ceana blocked her path and shoved the torch out in front of her. Caillic's sleeve caught fire.

Caillic screamed and dropped to the floor, smothering her sleeve in the dirt of the floor. Tears ran down her cheeks.

"Ceana." Gavran's voice was sharp, as if he wanted to tell her to stop but was also afraid to undermine her in front of Caillic. Even though the brollachan had released its control on her temporarily, it was still there somewhere, no doubt listening and watching everything that happened.

Ceana's stomach lurched, and saliva flooded her mouth. She hadn't meant to set Caillic on fire. Shoving the torch in front of her had been an instinctive motion. The words to defend herself, to reassure Gavran, rushed onto her tongue, but she clamped her lips shut.

Later. She'd have to explain it to him later. The best thing she could do now was exploit the accident, even if it did make her feel like she'd swallowed sludge.

The flames that had been creeping up the wall reached the roof in a whoosh, sped across, and stretched fingers down the opposite wall. The heat in the room turned oppressive.

Caillic looked up at her from where she crouched on the floor, cradling her arm. Her eyes flickered in the firelight—darkness filling them, then receding.

A shiver traced up Ceana's neck and down over her arms. She swallowed hard. She couldn't falter now. She firmed her grip on the torch. "I warned you."

"And I warned you." The voice coming from Caillic's mouth belonged to the brollachan again, deeper with an edge of rust.

Caillic crumpled to the floor.

Ceana jerked forward towards her then stopped. Was it a trick to get her to come close enough for the brollachan to wrestle the torch away from her? It was too late now. She couldn't stop the fire even if she wanted to. The small amount of water in the bucket wouldn't put out the flames spiderwebbing across the ceiling.

Caillic didn't move. Surely the brollachan wouldn't have killed her. The reason it gave for not coming after them once it found out the kelpie's fate was that it liked possessing Caillic.

Maybe not kill her then but abandon her? With a plan to come back later and reclaim her. That was a big risk if so. The brollachan couldn't be sure now that Ceana and Gavran wouldn't leave Caillic to burn. They wouldn't of course, but the brollachan couldn't read their minds. It couldn't be certain.

Gavran let out a pained grunt.

Ceana swiveled toward him and frowned. The flames had licked towards the door as well, but Gavran wasn't in danger from them yet. He held onto the doorframe with the same hand that clutched the *sgian*, and he'd hunched over slightly.

He sucked in a gasp of air. "Something hit me."

Hit him? Was the brollachan trying to escape through the doorway? Maybe it had planned to abandon Caillic to her fate after all. But if that were the case, couldn't it have gone through the walls? It was a disembodied spirit after all.

Unless the fire prevented it.

A force slammed into Ceana. She stumbled sideways, tripped over the bucket, and landed hard. Pain shot through her elbow.

The torch launched from her hand and rolled across the floor. It snuffed out.

The brollachan must be attacking them, but how was that possible? It didn't have physical form without possessing a body.

Caillic pushed herself into a sitting position with stiff, painful-looking movements. Nay, not stiff. Unnatural. The brollachan was back in control.

Caillic clambered to her feet and wailed.

Ceana scrambled after the torch. Her elbow and her ribs throbbed, but she had to reach it before Caillic did. It was her only option for a weapon.

"Servants of the Almighty." The brollachan's voice was sharp coming out of Caillic's lips again. "Servants of the Almighty. Get out. Get out. Get out."

Those shoves against her and Gavran—the brollachan wasn't attacking them physically. It'd been trying to possess them, hoping to force them to let it leave. That was the only thing that made sense of its wailing. And it hadn't been able to because they belonged to the Almighty. If they got out of this alive, she was going to have a discussion with the priest from Duntulm. Perhaps knowing that a demon couldn't enter into someone where the spirit of the Lord God already lived would embolden him to try helping Caillic again, even if he did think she'd welcomed the demon in. There had to be some way to free her. No one should have to live like this.

The roof crackled and snapped overhead. An ember shot down and bit into Ceana's hand. She whacked it away and grabbed the cool end of the torch.

The air had turned thick and hazy. Her lungs struggled to take it in, and her eyes watered. This had gone so much further than she ever intended. She had to get to the door and fresh air or she'd die here. The brollachan had reached the point where it might not mind being dispatched to Tartaros if it could take her with it.

Gavran called her name. She crawled towards him, trying to stay as far from the flames as possible, keeping the torch with her just in case. She reached the door. Gavran pulled her to her feet.

Caillic appeared out of the haze. Her eyes were wide. "Let me out."

Was the voice Caillic's or the brollachan's? With the smoke roughening all their throats, it could be either.

Gavran stepped to the side, almost making enough room for her to pass. Ceana grabbed his arm. He stiffened. He didn't have to speak for her to know what he'd be thinking. Were they really going to sacrifice Caillic? They couldn't cross that line.

The roof groaned. The brollachan would be feeling the heat and more. It'd be feeling the weight of fear on Caillic's chest, the fear that had kept it from lighting so much as a candle, and now the house was burning around it, the ceiling moments from collapsing in on it and its host.

Ceana planted her feet more firmly. She'd gamble that the brollachan would break before that happened. "Give me the information we bartered for, and I'll let you pass."

Caillic's form trembled. "Deal. Deal. Let me out."

With a fae, the promise was as good as having the information in hand. Once spoken, the brollachan couldn't go back on their deal.

A crack like thunder came from overhead. Gavran yanked Ceana backward and outside. She tripped over her own feet, but he kept them moving. The brollachan shot out of the house on their heels.

CHAPTER 12

*C*eana glanced back over her shoulder as she, Gavran, and the brollachan stumbled through the clearing away from the cottage. The roof collapsed with a rush, and sparks shot high in the air like geysers.

Almighty help her, if anyone saw this fire, she'd have no excuse. She had set this fire. Any destruction would be her fault.

The brollachan kept Caillic's body moving long past the searing heat of the flames. Finally, the brollachan slowed and turned back to face them.

Soot streaked Caillic's features. In any other situation, that might have made her look vulnerable. But the blown-wide pupils staring back at Ceana were definitely the brollachan's influence.

Ceana's bruises and minor burns ached. Beside her, Gavran bent over, panting.

But the brollachan glared at them with posture more perfect than a lady's and even breathing. The last shred of doubt that the brollachan was fully back in control of Caillic's body evaporated.

Ceana's mouth dried out as if she'd eaten ash. She swallowed hard. If it wanted revenge on them now, it could take it. They weren't in any shape to fight. Everything depended on whether it considered their deal binding or not.

"The MacLeod fairy." The brollachan spat the words as if they were viler than the raw meat it'd been eating before they'd interrupted it.

Ceana's vision spun. She softened her knees to keep them from giving out on her. The brollachan was going to give them the name after all. This was finally going to be over.

The thought pinged around in her head and refused to settle. Had she not truly believed it until this moment? Been afraid to believe it maybe. They'd been chasing freedom from the curses for so long that to have the solution about to be set in her palm… Her chest went tight, and her eyes burned.

Gavran straightened slightly, and the silence stretched.

"The MacLeod fairy's name is?" Gavran said.

One side of Caillic's mouth twitched up in a farce of a smile. She rolled her head side to side in the way anyone else might to loosen their neck. "The MacLeod fairy. That's my part of our deal. Paid in full."

Ceana shook her head slightly. The words made no sense, like a message spoken under water. There had to be a misunderstanding. "That's not a name. Our bargain was for the name of the fairy who cursed us."

The brollachan made a huffing sound through its nose. Its version of a laugh? "No, mortal. The bargain we made was for information. You said you would let me pass in exchange for the information we originally bartered for. And our original deal was not for a name. *You will free an enslaved kelpie for me. In exchange, I will give you information.* That was the original deal."

A buzzing noise filled Ceana's ears, then her whole head. She couldn't remember the exact words they'd used. But the brollachan couldn't lie to her about their deal. The nature of the fae prevented it. And the fae were nothing if not good at spinning what a person thought was said into something else entirely.

They'd made a deal that allowed the brollachan too much leeway, and she'd missed it. Information. A name. In her mind, they'd meant the same thing. But they weren't. Not even close. And, of course, the brollachan would use any crack they'd left it, especially now.

Its own perfect form of revenge.

The brollachan leaned forward slightly. "Our dealings are now complete. If you value your lives, I suggest you never try to seek me or any of my kind out again. We will not forget."

The air cut off slowly to Ceana's lungs, as if a snake had wrapped around her neck and was squeezing her life out. As if not getting the fairy's name weren't bad enough, now they'd made an enemy of an entire branch of demons.

"Please." Gavran's voice was pulled taunt. "Show mercy if you have any. Give us the name. You know that's what we intended from the bargain."

Ceana's chest ached. Her Gavran. Still hoping. Still hoping despite everything he'd seen that there was some tiny speck of good in this creature that he could appeal to.

"I didn't intend for my brethren to end up dead. And after what she tried to do to me?" The brollachan pointed at Ceana. "Mercy?" The brollachan fully laughed this time. The sound was harsh rather than cheerful. "No mercy. I know which fairy you seek, and before night falls, she'll know you're seeking her. She will relish hunting you down. You can call upon her mercy, and maybe she'll kill you quickly. That's the only kind of mercy you'll receive."

The brollachan spun, and ran off into the trees at a pace that a normal human being couldn't have managed.

A wave of exhaustion flooded over Ceana's body. That was it then. No name. No way to get the fairy's name. And the fairy would soon be coming to stop them from even trying.

She should have done as Gavran asked. They should have given up trying to break free from the cursed wishes. They wouldn't have been able to live the kind of life they'd wanted, but maybe she could have figured out a half-life that they could have been satisfied with, if not content.

Now what was the point of any of what they'd done? The fairy would hunt them down and likely torture Gavran in front of her to punish her. Because for a reason she still didn't know, the fairy hadn't been willing to let them die a simple death by drowning.

A strong hand slid into hers and pulled her close. Gavran's arms wrapped around her and held tight, swaddling her in his embrace.

"I've got you," he whispered.

She leaned against him. Drew in a long, slow breath. Her heartbeat ticked down one notch. Another breath, another slight easing of the frantic pounding in her ears.

Had Gavran realized she was unraveling? He'd seen it happen enough times. Seen her ready to give up when they hit an obstacle like this.

She wrapped her hands in the fabric of his shirt. Sliding back into her old ways had been too easy. That wasn't who she wanted to be anymore. She didn't want to be that person who found her path blocked by a wall and who sat down and waited to die. She wanted to be the kind of person who held onto hope to find a way around or over or under. Who held on until her fingers were bloody from scrabbling and her body gave out. Who took the wall apart piece by piece if necessary.

A person who persevered until the end. *Lord God, let me be that brave.*

She wouldn't lie down in the grass and let the darkness take her the way she wanted to. Not this time.

She sucked in one more breath and pulled back. "Well, that didn't work the way I imagined."

Gavran laughed. It had a slightly crazy edge to it. "Nay. Nor I."

She might have only a few days or a few hours left once the

fairy found out. She could find enough courage for that amount of time and worry about the rest later. "We have more than we did before. The MacLeod fairy."

Gavran kissed her forehead and gave her a look that made her feel like she was actually worth everything she'd put him through. "It might even be enough. Lady MacDonald might know the name of the MacLeod fairy."

~

CEANA BIT DOWN on her bottom lip until it ached while Gavran told Salome everything that had happened to them since they'd parted.

Salome lowered herself into a chair and pressed a hand to her ever-growing stomach. "Maeve might know."

Ceana released her bottom lip with a pop. So Salome didn't know herself, but she knew someone who might. Someone she trusted enough to mention to them. Surely she wouldn't give then false hope. Not after everything they'd been through. "Where can we find her? Can you summon her here?"

Salome's gaze shifted in her direction. "That's the problem. You'll have to travel to her, and she'll not be happy to see you. Maeve is the spaewife you met in Dunvegan."

Ceana's heart hit hard against the front of her chest, then sank.

Gavran made a choking noise followed by a coughing fit. "Met. Accosted is more like. Ceana knocked the air from her lungs. I held a *sgian* on her. We were arguing about whether or not to kill her when she got loose and cried for help."

Tension bloomed into thorned roses above Ceana's eyebrows. She rubbed the tips of her fingers into them. Forcing information about Salome from Maeve the spaewife felt like it'd been years ago. So much had happened. From their perspective at least.

From Maeve's, it'd only been weeks. She wouldn't have

forgotten them. She certainly wouldn't have any reason to trust or help them. "There's nothing you can tell us instead? Even if Maeve would help us, we might not make it there. The fairy won't want us to, and she knows what we're doing now or she soon will."

Salome used both hands to push herself from her chair. She moved to the fireplace. Only coals remained in it, but Salome stretched her hands towards it despite the summer heat. "If I'd heard of this fairy while living as a selkie, she wouldn't have been called the MacLeod fairy among the seelie. We would have used her name." She turned her back to the fireplace but didn't move away from it. "The seelie don't spend time gossiping or spreading tales. It serves no purpose. Our time is taken up with our service to the Lord God."

In other words, Maeve was their best chance, if not their only chance, of figuring out the fairy's name. "She's not going to help us. She might report us to the MacLeod guards without even listening to us."

Salome rested her hands on top of her belly. She hadn't been doing that before they'd left to seek the brollachan. "She might. If I ask her. Maeve was a dear friend to me at a time when I most needed one. I was the one who sent her to Dunvegan to protect her. When I first became fully human, I didn't know what the unseelie might do to try to force me to break my promises."

Sending Maeve away had been wise. As it was, the unseelie had sent the nuckalevee that tormented the people under the MacDonalds' protection until she and Gavran had killed it.

"Forgive me, my lady," Gavran said. "But Lord MacDonald won't allow you to travel."

Ceana glanced in his direction. Red streaked his neck at even the oblique reference to Salome's condition.

Salome smiled slightly. "I can't go with you. I'll have to send a message to Maeve that she will know could only have come from me."

She went to the fireplace hearth and brought down a small bottle. She placed it into Ceana's hands.

Ceana held it up to the light. The liquid inside was blue and full of sediment. The glass of the bottle held no marking. It could have come from anywhere. From anyone. "She'll know this is from you?"

Salome nodded her head once. "It's a message that can't be forged. And last we spoke, I hadn't yet learned to write. She wouldn't recognize my hand if I were to send a missive with you now."

Ceana's heart beat in her chest like a rabbit thumping its back leg. "And how will we get halfway across the isle without the fairy stopping us."

Salome's smile grew. "That, I think, is going to take a wagonload of iron."

CHAPTER 13

Sweat dripped down the side of Ceana's neck and was sopped up by her already drenched leine. The throbbing in her hip from lying for hours in one position on the hard, wooden bed of the wagon was near unbearable. She shifted position. The rounded edge of a horse shoe jabbed her in the shoulder blade.

"I thought Salome was teasing us when she said we'd need a wagonload of iron," Gavran said from where he lay across from her. He poked at the tarpaulin secured overtop of them. "It'd be more bearable without this thing. Do you think it even matters? If a fairy can pass through walls, I'd imagine she could see through fabric."

She had no argument for him. The material wasn't even thick enough to block out all the light. Though, if it had been, they'd have likely suffocated. As it was, the air was thick enough that she had to force down every breath as if she were swallowing soup.

The wagon turned right again, and Ceana rolled backwards, the horseshoe and something that felt like the buckle for a saddle girth jabbing her again. The bruises on her back must look like a reverse of the stars in the night sky by this point, all points of black on her pale skin.

Gavran wiped a sleeve across his forehead and frowned. "How many right turns has that been since we left Duntulm Castle?"

Ceana closed her eyes. They'd crept into the stables before the sun even peeked over the horizon, cloaks hiding them from watching eyes, human or otherwise, and crawled into the wagon bed that Lord MacDonald and Eachann had prepared for them. A maidservant and groom had worn the cloaks back into the castle. A weak way of tricking the fairy if she'd already been watching them, but better than nothing.

Ceana hadn't slept well leading up to their flight, and she was sure she'd slipped into sleep more than once in the hours of travel. But they shouldn't have made any sharp right turns until tomorrow morn at the earliest, when they had to go around the loch that cut deep into the isle, let alone multiple times if Gavran were correct.

"Eachann?" She kept her voice soft.

"Metal doesn't speak," the equally soft reply came back. "And you can't possibly need to stop yet."

They'd stopped only a few hours past for them to each run into the bushes, clothing stuffed full of nails in the hope that might be enough to protect them if the fairy showed up. Then they'd crawled right back under the tarpaulin with a flask of water and the bread and dried meat Cook had packed for them.

Gavran edged toward the front of the wagon, and his knee connected with a shield. He sucked in a breath. "Have you turned us around for some reason?"

"You must have been dreaming. We've been on a straight path since we left Duntulm."

Gavran's gaze connected with hers. A knot more painful than

the ones in her back and hip formed in her stomach. Eachann wouldn't lie to them. He hadn't wanted to come with them and abandon his post as Salome's guard, but he'd volunteered anyway when Lord MacDonald shared Salome's plan. This mission was too dangerous, he'd argued, for them to send anyone else. They'd have to tell their driver of the risks, and that would mean too great a chance of exposure for Salome.

Ceana wriggled slightly closer to Gavran, being careful not to bump into anything the way he had. "Do you know how many times we've turned?"

Gavran shook his head. "I thought we were avoiding downed trees or boulders at first."

Her mouth went even drier than it already was. "But you're certain?"

Gavran nodded. "It started happening after our last stop."

Everything inside her spooled tight enough to snap. The curses she'd heard during her time living in Dunvegan's back alleys after the wishes took over her life didn't seem fierce enough. She slapped a hand into the bed of the wagon hard enough to make her palm sting. "She's found us."

"Either that, or Eachann's betrayed us."

Would the second option be the better of the two? Someone they'd trusted turning on them? Any person not off their head would surely prefer that. A human betraying them was easier to overcome than a supernatural predator finding them. But her mind shied away from it. She'd rather face the fairy than a betrayal by a friend.

How they handled this would be very different depending on which option turned out to be truth.

She whispered a prayer for wisdom. A certainty settled deep down in her soul, too deep to have come from herself. She had to trust those who'd earned it. "It's not Eachann."

Gavran stuck a hand out the front of the wagon bed and

released one of the ties, then another, then another. A breeze caught the tarpaulin, and it flapped up. The afternoon summer air that would have normally scorched her caressed her skin like a balm instead.

Eachann glanced back. "Stay down. I'll stop and fasten it back in place."

Ceana sat up. Gavran followed her more slowly. He massaged a fist into his lower back.

Eachann pulled on the reins. The oxen slowed their steps until the wagon finally rolled to a stopped. "Are you *eejits*? I didn't spend my day watching the hind ends of these beasts just so you could get yourselves killed rather than continue to sweat."

A shiver coursed down Ceana's skin, and it was only half due to the change in temperature. The fairy could be watching them right now. Listening. But what other choice did they have. If they were right, they could travel for weeks without coming any closer to Dunvegan, until they ran out of food and the oxen collapsed from fatigue.

"You've been driving in circles."

"Did the heat make you cracked up here?" Eachann tapped his temple.

However the fairy had managed to turn them in circles, she'd done it in a way that blinded Eachann to what was happening. The fae liked games. The fairy must be toying with them before killing them. Watching them exhaust themselves first must be giving her some sort of twisted pleasure.

Gavran pointed to the left. "Nay? Then how do you explain that?"

Eachann frowned and shifted his gaze. Ceana did as well. In the distance, the horizon line stretched blue and sparkling. Eachann blinked rapidly as if he couldn't decide whether he was seeing a mirage as well or not.

He turned to look to the right, where the water should have been if they'd still been heading for Dunvegan. He rubbed a fist across his eyes. "I don't understand. Until you pointed the water out to me and forced me to stare at it, I would have sworn an oath that it was on the other side."

Ceana swallowed hard. "She's making you see things. There's no point in hiding anymore. We need to turn around and keep moving. And all of us need to watch the water."

CHAPTER 14

One of the oxen stumbled, and Eachann eased back on the reins. "We have to rest them. Are we at least facing in the right direction? I can't tell anymore."

Ceana looked both directions. Trees on the left, as they should be. Water on the right. "Aye. We're facing toward Dunvegan."

For all the good it would do them. The circle they'd been treading was close to a kilometer in length, if the landmarks she'd taken note of were any indication. Yet after traveling all day and partway into the night, they were still stuck halfway between Dunvegan and Duntulm.

Or maybe her own eyes were playing her false. She glanced at Gavran.

He shook his head. "I can't tell either. It's like looking into a mirage, there one minute and gone the next."

"And wavering." Eachann laid the reins on his knees. The oxen had stopped, and their heads drooped. "I think I see the water on one side, then it's on my other."

Ceana frowned. She looked around again, more slowly this time. The world wasn't changing around her the way Eachann and Gavran experienced it. She always knew which side the water was on, and it stayed put, until the moment when she looked up and it wasn't on the side she'd marked before and she couldn't remember turning.

Once the sun had begun to set and she could feel the heat shift from one side of her face to the other, she'd known the instant the switch happened.

A sound half laughter and half the crack of ice breaking up in the spring echoed around them. "It's the weak and fickle nature of men's minds. I did try to warn you."

A figure materialized on the road in front of the oxen. Her edges wavered like she was more a reflection on water than real flesh and blood. Long rust-red hair, the same shade as Ceana's own, flowed around her, held back on either side with silver combs shaped like tangled spider webs. The woman's white dress glowed in contrast to her long forest-green cloak.

Blood rushed to Ceana's head, and her skin burned. Even if she hadn't been watching for her, she would have known who she was facing.

This was the fairy who'd cursed them.

Ceana stood in the wagon, making sure that she stayed in the middle of the nest of iron. She touched her skirt. A heavy bag of nails still hung from her waist. She was as protected as she would ever have a chance to be.

But Eachann wasn't. She had to distract the fairy long enough for him to climb into the back of the wagon with them.

"They're not the ones who hurt me." She kept her hands by her sides but poked a finger in Eachann's direction, then tried to motion backward. "That was you."

Gavran's gaze barely flickered towards her fingers. Did he understand or was he thinking she was twitching from fear? She couldn't even look at him in any significant way. She couldn't risk drawing the fairy's attention to what she was doing.

"I've been the one helping you." The fairy's voice had that eerily soft yet carrying quality that Ceana remembered from their one and only meeting. Her voice seemed to be everywhere at once without being loud. "I'm trying to teach you valuable lessons you need. You chose to learn them the hard way. I gave you a different option."

Gavran's expression shifted subtly beside her, and he eased forward. He closed two fingers around the back of Eachann's leine and tugged. Eachann shrugged his shoulders as if he thought he'd gotten caught on something.

The fairy's gaze moved to Eachann.

Almighty save them. She had to get the fairy's attention back on her. "I learned. Your cur—wishes let me know how strong I can be on my own. But I don't want to live this way forever."

The fairy made a tutting sound. "You never had to, my dear. I thought you were smarter than this. You should have figured it out by now."

Her heart fluttered in her chest. She never had to live like this? She tamped the hope down before it could rise any higher. There would be a catch. This wasn't a deal she would want to make any more than she'd wanted to take the fairy's original "gift."

But the longer she could keep the fairy talking, the better chance they had of getting Eachann safely back among the iron with them. "I'm sorry I've disappointed you. But I would like to be released now. That's the only reason I was seeking you out."

Maybe the fairy wouldn't know it was a lie. It had enough truth in it. The brollachan hadn't known why they wanted the fairy's name after all.

The fairy smiled at her. It was so warm and motherly that Ceana had to stop herself from taking a step toward her and out of the safety of the iron-filled wagon bed.

Gavran tugged again at Eachann's leine. Eachann went unnaturally still, as if more statue than man.

"I was trying to protect you, child. So all you have to do is prove you've learned the lesson I was teaching you, and you will no longer be under the power of the wishes." The fairy's smile was a little too high on one side, and her gaze landed hard on Gavran. "All you have to do is kill him."

Ceana sucked in a breath. Her vision tunneled in on the fairy, and she couldn't see anymore if Eachann was moving or if Gavran was still trying to convey their message.

Eliezer had hypothesized that the cursed wishes might break if Gavran died. The balance would be upset, and there'd be no counterbalance to what she received. It was one of the arguments that Gavran had made in favor of them marrying and living within the walls of Duntulm Castle. He wanted to wager that if he died, the cursed wishes would lift, and she would be able to take care of any children they had.

But this…

"What if I die naturally or by another's hand?" Gavran's voice had something in it that she couldn't pick apart, like threads of a wet fabric that had swollen together too tightly to be separated, short of cutting them.

She bit her bottom lip to keep from looking at him. Surely he couldn't be considering what his question implied. Surely he was attempting to distract the fairy from any movement by Eachann, just as she'd been doing.

Because she'd wouldn't allow it. Not even as a final resort.

"By her hand only." The fairy's tone was sweeter than honey.

Ceana glanced at Gavran. His shoulders hollowed. She forced her arms to stay pressed by her sides instead of reaching for him. She'd been right, but there was no pleasure in it. Had they wed and he'd died, she'd have been trapped in the cycle of the cursed wishes forever. Had she found her brother, had she and Gavran had children, she would have had to live her worst fears realized. She'd have lost not only him with his passing, but all of them.

Eachann tipped backward as if trying to tumble into the wagon bed with them. Gavran grabbed for his arms, but before he could make contact with him, Eachann was gone.

CHAPTER 15

Gavran pitched forward, and Ceana lunged toward him. She caught his arm and threw her body backwards before he could fall out of the safety of the wagon bed.

Her tail bone hit the wood and sharp pain lanced through her limbs. Gavran came down half on her and half onto the wagon bed. Thank the good Lord neither of them had landed on the swords or other iron packing the wagon bed.

She breathed through the pain, pushing it to the back of her mind. Eachann. What had happened to Eachann?

Her body fought her as she tried to move. Her side felt wet. Had she stabbed herself after all? Where was the pain? She reached a hand down and raised her fingers. Damp but not red. She pressed a hand to the spot. Shards dug into her hip and her palm.

Salome's bottle. The message to Maeve. She'd smashed it when she fell.

They'd have to figure out if they could salvage it somehow. She dragged herself sideways until she reached the box board.

Eachann stood next to the rutted wagon path, the fairy at his side. He towered over her, the top of her head only reaching his shoulder, but it was clear she was in control. He stood as stiff as if someone had strapped boards to all his limbs. He likely wasn't able to move. Only his gaze snapped from the fairy to the wagon and back again.

The fairy smiled directly at Ceana but said nothing.

Gavran shifted aside a shield and took its place beside Ceana. His breathing was fast.

She dug her fingernails into the wood. There was no way out of this. They'd been royal *eejits* to agree to Eachann coming along. They should have taken the risk of simply filling their pockets with nails and trying to sneak their way to Dunvegan. How would she ever be able to face Salome and Lord MacDonald again if something happened to Eachann? How would she be able to live with herself?

"Let him go." She forced as much courage and defiance into her voice as she could manage. "He's nothing to do with this."

The fairy tilted her head to one side in a way that was almost bird-like. Almost beautiful in its grace. "He tried to deceive me. That has made him part of it." Her gaze firmed slightly, the way Ceana's mamaidh's had right before she delivered a lecture. "Deceitfulness is part of men's natures. He'll need to be punished for his transgression so he learns the consequences of falsehood."

Was that…pain in the fairy's tone? Ceana gripped the wood so tightly splinters burrowed into her palms. The fairy seemed to take Eachann's aid of them personally. Like Eachann helping them was done to intentionally hurt her.

Ceana's throat seized. Whatever the fairy planned to do as punishment, it would be cruel. That wasn't in question. Eachann might not even survive it.

She had to stop it. But how?

Her mind turned blank as a hard-pressed stretch of road, where not even a weed managed to grow. What if she couldn't stop it?

The air came out of her lungs, and spots bounced at the edges of her vision. A warm hand settled firmly on her back.

"Breathe," Gavran whispered.

She didn't want to breathe. Losing consciousness might be better. She wouldn't have to watch.

She swallowed and sucked in a breath. That would be the coward's way out. Eachann couldn't escape this. Neither should she.

The fairy swung herself up on a fallen tree, crossed her ankles, and twirled her fingers. Her expression had the half-smile and calm intensity of someone awaiting the start of an anticipated performance.

Eachann hopped on the ball of one foot, kicking the other leg out, then pirouetting around, only to repeat the pattern on the other side, his feet dragging him along in dance steps to silent music. Music that perhaps not even Eachann could hear, though the fairy surely could, based on how she bounced a foot in time with his movements.

Gavran leaned close and placed his lips against her ear. "This won't hold her interest long. Perhaps she'll let him go soon enough."

Ceana rested her arms along the top of the box board. Aye, the fairy might lose interest. How long could she possibly enjoy watching Eachann dance. But then what? She might come up with something far worse.

The moon dropped an hour's worth in the sky, then another, all of them sitting in a silent tableau except for Eachann. The stoicism drained from his face, replaced by pain he couldn't hide.

Every grimace on his face was a kick in Ceana's gut. Gavran had laid his forehead against the box board a half hour past, though his occasional shifting suggested he was still awake and simply unable to bear watching anymore. The fairy hadn't tired of her game.

All the tales she'd ever heard about the fae making humans dance until they died played on repeat in her head.

Pinks streaked the horizon, and still Eachann danced and the fairy watched.

The fairy lifted one finger, and Eachann leaped into the air, twirling around. He landed, but his ankle bent, and he cried out. His legs gave way beneath him. He collapsed to the ground.

Gavran's head jerked up, and he straightened his back. His posture screamed that he believed it was finally over. That the fairy would have exacted enough punishment.

The urge to slap him and to kiss him warred inside her. Even all they'd faced hadn't been able to shake loose the hope he clung to like a bairn. What did he think was going to happen next? She'd been turning them in circles for hours. Surely Eachann's punishment was only the beginning.

"She's seelie." Gavran spoke the words so softly that she couldn't be sure if he was speaking to her or to himself. "Lady MacDonald was sure she's seelie. She'll have to stop now."

He glanced at her as if seeking confirmation.

She had no reassurance to give him. After what the fairy had done to them—to her—would she stop simply because Eachann was injured? She hadn't intervened all the times Ceana had been beaten. All the times she'd bled. All the times unspeakable things had been done to her.

The fairy lifted her hand into the air, palm up, and Eachann rose to his feet like a puppet pulled by invisible strings.

His feet moved back into the jig he'd been doing prior to his fall. Every time his left foot connected with the ground, he gasped. His face turned paler and paler until he looked coated in a layer of dust.

"She's seelie." Gavran repeated to himself like a prayer. "She's seelie."

"Stop!" The word ripped from Ceana's chest without conscious thought. "Please!"

The fairy turned her face in Ceana's direction. "Are you offering to take his place?"

"Nay," Eachann and Gavran said at the same time.

The fairy shook her head slowly, scoldingly. "You are only proving my point once again by trying to speak for her."

Eachann dropped to the ground, still at last.

The fairy smiled at Ceana, but there was a challenge to it. "What is your answer to my question?"

A tremble shivered down Ceana's body and stayed in her hands and legs. It was a trick. Again. If she offered herself up in Eachann's place, she'd be sacrificing herself for a man the way she'd done for Gavran back when all this started. The fairy would take it as proof that she hadn't learned her lesson. She might even come up with another way to try to teach it to her. She might force them to stay in this wagon, surrounded by the iron that prevented her from touching them, until they died of thirst.

But the alternative seemed to be to sit here and watch Eachann dance himself to death.

Beside her, Gavran's breathing was ragged. He watched her, his gaze a caress. He knew. He knew what she wanted to do. And what the consequences of either decision might do to her.

"I choose to stay here." The words hurt coming out, as if her teeth were being yanked out along with them. "But I'm asking you to show pity. He may have deceived you, but he did it out of loyalty to me and to another woman who asked for his aid."

The sun lifted high enough that it cast one side of the fairy's face into light, her features sharp and alive, and left the other in shadows.

The fairy rose from the tree and turned to face Ceana directly. The stark contrast of the light shifted with her movement, covering her whole face in the soft light of dawn. Her eyes, her cheekbones, her lips—one moment she was so stunning she put the sunrise to shame and then the next so plain she could have blended into any crowd.

Ceana blinked hard. She'd always been able to see the ugliness of the unseelie, and Gavran had often been blinded by the beautiful mask they covered it over with. But the unseelie were never ordinary or plain. Perhaps their pride prevented it. Perhaps they knew beauty would play on people's natural biases to immediately make them more liked and trusted and able to deceive. Whatever the reason, the being standing before her, torturing Eachann, couldn't be unseelie. The fairy had to be seelie. The ordinariness of her features settled the truth deep in Ceana's bones.

It made no sense.

The fairy tilted her head to one side slightly, and the smile she gave Ceana was soft. "Your heart is too gentle for this world, my child." The edges of her lips hardened. "Don't make me take you from it or do something else you won't properly appreciate in order to protect you. I will let this one go for now." She waved a hand dismissively at Eachann. "But this is your final warning. Stop seeking for me. I will not take back the gift I bestowed upon you. You know now how simple it is to free yourself." She turned her gaze onto Gavran. "All you have to do is kill him."

CHAPTER 16

*T*he fairy disappeared, and Ceana launched herself from the wagon and sprinted for Eachann.

"Wait." Gavran leaped over the side after her. "It could be a trick. She might not be gone."

She dropped to the ground next to Eachann. Gavran joined her. "She can't lie."

Eachann lay flat on his back, gasping in deep gulping breathes, his sides heaving like a horse who'd run two races across the moors back to back. "She can't lie." Eachann laughed, but it turned into a cough. "But seems to me she can do most anything else."

Ceana refused to look at Gavran. His question to the fairy about the ways he could die that would free her from the cursed wishes still echoed in her ears.

"Come on," Gavran said. "We need to get you to the wagon."

Eachann let Gavran help him to a sitting position, but then pushed his hands away. "I'm not sure I can walk."

Ceana glanced at Eachann's boots. The soles were worn through as if he'd been dancing for weeks instead of hours. Maybe there was some truth to the tales about humans losing time in the fairy realm. "We should take a look at your ankle then?"

She couldn't stop the words from turning into a question. She couldn't bear it if what they did now caused Eachann further injury. This was all her fault.

Nay. The rebellion rose up slowly inside her, then built like a wave at sea before it crashed on the shore. She'd made many mistakes, but she didn't bear the guilt this time, even though Eachann had come along for her sake. All the guilt lay on the fairy's scales for this. She could have left Eachann out of it. She could have removed the cursed wishes and brought it all to an end.

Gavran moved to Eachann's feet. "Lyall showed me how to check bones. I might be able to tell if the injury's in the muscle or deeper."

Eachann propped his arms behind him, leaned back slightly, and closed his eyes. "It's the left one."

Gavran worked the laces of Eachann's boot free. The knots seemed to take twice as long as normal to untie, and Gavran loosened the laces as far as they would go. He motioned Ceana closer. "Will you hold his ankle steady for me?"

She braced both her hands under Eachann's ankle, preparing to take its weight as the boot slid free. Gavran eased the boot half a finger's length. Eachann sucked in a gasp.

Gavran froze.

Eachann's jaw tensed. "Keep going. It can't be worse than when I cut off your toe, and you survived that." A hint of teasing laced his tone despite the strain.

Ceana drew a breath deep into her lungs. She hadn't realized how shallowly she'd been breathing. Eachann didn't blame them either, though she wouldn't have been wroth with him if he had.

Gavran tugged and wiggled until Eachann's boot came off, the lines in Gavran's forehead growing deeper with every grunt from Eachann. The boot fell to the ground.

Ceana kept her hands supporting Eachann's ankle through a sheer act of will. His foot was soaked in blood, blisters tearing open his flesh at more points than she could count.

He must have been in agony long before he showed a sign.

She met Gavran's gaze.

"I'll grab a cloak from the wagon to support his ankle." Gavran leaned back on his heels. "Then I think we ought to take the other boot off as well."

Eachann heaved a sigh. "I was hoping it wasn't as bad as it felt."

Gavran came running back with two cloaks and a bottle of wine. He balled one of the cloaks up under Eachann's ankle, then pulled out his *sgian* and cut long strips of cloth off the second cloak.

Ceana gently removed Eachann's second boot while Gavran worked. Eachann was looking up at the sky, a pinched quality to his face like he was trying to keep himself from passing out.

"I can't say if it's worse than it feels," she said. Eachann's gaze snapped to her face. "But at least you didn't give her the satisfaction of seeing it."

Eachann barked out a laugh.

Ceana wanted to fake one along with him for his sake, but she couldn't manage it. *She's seelie*, Gavran had kept repeating. He'd been hoping she'd still prove herself good. But what she'd done to Eachann was anything but good. Setting up the wishes so that the only way to free herself was to kill Gavran was anything but good. The fairy was not good.

"Ready?" Gavran asked.

EVEN WITH THE leather in his mouth, Eachann couldn't hold back a scream. It ripped through Gavran, but he kept pouring until the last drop of wine was gone. Ceana's mamaidh used to pack wounds with honey to keep infection away, but they hadn't passed a hive that he could remember. "This'll be the best we can do until we can get back to Lyall."

Eachann sucked in air through his teeth. "At least my feet won't rot off while we drive in circles for her amusement."

Perhaps. The fairy hadn't actually promised to leave them alone if they returned to Duntulm. She'd only said she'd let Eachann go for now and had admonished them to stop seeking her. That was the kind of speech fae gave that could get a man into trouble. It sounded one way right up until they showed you that what they meant by it was something only a twisted mind could conceive of.

But Eachann didn't need that worry weighing him down when he'd need all his strength to get back to Duntulm at all.

Gavran checked Eachann's left ankle the way Lyall had described, then compared it to the bones in his own. Everything felt normal, praise be to the Almighty. And thanks to Ceana for convincing the fairy to stop.

Gavran handed her a piece of the cloak he'd torn into bindings. The dust from the road clung to it, but it was cleaner than anything else they had.

She carefully wound the cloth around Eachann's right foot. Blood and wine seeped through the first layer of wrappings.

Her hands shook slightly. "How could the fairy be seelie? Salome said she must still believe she was working for the Almighty. But how could anyone do something so cruel and believe they were working for the Almighty? What she did to Eachann. What she did to us. To me."

Her voice was tight and broken at the same time.

He wanted to wrap her up in his arms and hide her away from all the hurt and dangers in the world, but some things he couldn't protect her from no matter how much he wanted to. He couldn't erase the past.

Why did anyone who believed in the Lord God Almighty do evil? Some who claimed His name didn't really believe in or follow him, and so they brought shame to those who did through their falsehood. But that couldn't be the case with the fairy. According to Salome, if she were in rebellion against the Almighty—even secretly—she'd have lost her name and her place and the wishes wouldn't have helped them defeat the nuckalevee. The fairy had to truly believe she was serving the Almighty in her actions.

Ceana had lived the night when the fairy cursed them with the wishes only once. He'd lived it over and over, dreaming it every night until he and Ceana had reunited. He could probably repeat the speech she'd given word for word, inflection for inflection. There were doubtless things he remembered that Ceana didn't.

He wound a strip of cloth slowly around Eachann's foot, careful to apply the right amount of pressure. "The night she saved us, she sounded like she was trying to protect you from me. She thought I would use you, eventually betray you, and she wanted to spare you that. She wanted you to learn your lesson before it was too late." He grimaced. The fairy had seemed like a parody of motherly concern at times. "She called what she was doing a *gift*."

The fairy had said similar things today. Ceana could only prove she'd learned her lesson by killing him. The sharp stab in his chest hit him again. They had a way out if it came to it. If things ever got bad enough.

He stole a look at Ceana, bent over Eachann's foot, her bottom lip sucked in while she concentrated. The urge to drag her into his arms and kiss her flooded him. The fairy didn't know Ceana. She'd never do it. No matter how bad things got. No matter what the fairy did to her.

Ceana knotted off the fabric around Eachann's foot. "She said she tried to warn my mamaidh not to marry my dadaidh. She didn't want me repeating her mistake. Didn't she say something about other women?"

Even the heat of the day and the sweat trickling down his back couldn't stop the shiver that traced over his skin. The fairy had said that. "Like she thought she'd been trying to protect women from the abuses of men."

"That's probably what stopped her from having me dance until my blood all drained out my feet." Eachann's breathing was still labored. "You told her I acted in service to you and Lady MacDonald."

Gavran tied off the material on Eachann's left foot. They'd never be able to fit his feet back into his boots. The fairy's methods were wrong, no doubt. But if they guessed her motives correctly, she'd been doing all of it not to hurt, but in the mistaken belief she was helping. "Treating women well would please the Almighty if she hadn't gone about it the way she had."

"Who knows what things she's done to other women and other couples over the years. The decades. She needs to be stopped." Ceana whispered the words, but there was a firmness in them hard as the iron they'd packed themselves in for the journey. "Stopping her isn't just about us."

A lump built at the bottom of Gavran's throat. Had she been this brave and selfless before the wishes? She must have been to sacrifice herself for him. How could she have ever believed that he didn't love her? Her soul was so beautiful it far outshone all the flaws she saw in herself.

He shifted forward and captured her lips with his. She leaned into him, as if it were the most natural thing in the world.

"You deserve each other." Eachann's gruff tone cut through the haze building in his head at Ceana's touch. "You're both *eejits*. You're going after her, aren't you? Ignoring what she said."

Ceana pulled back from him. He snagged one more quick kiss before letting her go.

She smiled at Eachann, her lips pulling up in a way that was slightly manic. "It's the only way to end this. I won't let her do this to anyone else. And I won't live the rest of my life with her threats hanging over my head."

Gavran let out a breath. They had been threats, hadn't they? He hadn't heard them until Ceana pointed them out. But the fairy wanted her to kill him. That was the only acceptable proof that Ceana had learned her "lesson." The fairy wouldn't allow them to live in peace at Duntulm for long, even if they were willing to turn back and give up. She'd find a way to push them out, and she'd keep pushing.

Eachann stuck an arm out towards him. "Help me up. You'll need someone to drive you."

Gavran helped Eachann to his feet. Eachann leaned heavily on him and took a step, his full weight dragging on Gavran. He braced his knees until Eachann straightened.

The wagon hadn't seemed so far away before but now it might as well have been on the other side of the loch.

Ceana looped Eachann's other arm over her shoulder.

Step by aching step they got him back to the wagon. Working together, they hoisted him up into the driver's seat.

Sweat drenched Eachann's face, and there was a sharp edge to his breathing. "Get in." His words came out in a rasp.

They couldn't allow him to continue driving them to Dunvegan. Gavran reached for Ceana's hand. She entwined her fingers with his and squeezed. It must be the years of shared history held just outside his memory that let her understand him this way.

He squeezed back. "You're going to take the wagon back to Duntulm without us."

Eachann's jaw clenched. "I'm not. And the longer you stand there like practice dummies, the more likely that crazed fairy is to change her mind and come back."

He could argue with Eachann that the fairy might kill him the next time, but that seemed unlikely to work. The man was still insisting on going with them after all the fairy had done to him.

Whether it was pride or loyalty, either would be difficult to break.

"We need a distraction. We'll cover the wagon up like it was before and have you head back to Duntulm as if we were inside. We'll go the rest of the way to Dunvegan on foot, trying to stay under cover as much as we can. If you go back, it might buy us enough time."

CHAPTER 17

*T*he crowd wasn't as thick as it was on Dunvegan's market day, but enough people traveled back and forth across the square, moving wagons of hay, armloads of wood, and herding sheep that they wouldn't look suspicious as long as they kept moving.

Ceana touched the pouch of glass fragments again. No use wishing that they'd meld themselves back together again. Hopefully it hadn't been the liquid inside that would let Maeve known Salome sent them. Perhaps there was something about the glass itself, something Ceana couldn't see. And perhaps the pigs that they stopped to let pass would sprout wings too.

"It's strange being back." Gavran's voice was soft. "Last time we were here, we were fleeing from my dadaidh and Tavish."

If she squinted, blurring her vision, she could imagine she saw a crowded square and them dodging through it to escape. It hadn't only been Allan and Tavish after them. Maeve's screams had roused the MacLeod guards as well. Spaewives might not be respected, but they were needed.

Gavran pointed. "Her tent's still there at least."

Ceana looked to where he indicated. Maeve's double-belled

wedge tent was indeed still pitched in the same spot they'd last visited it weeks ago. Something tight in her chest released slightly. Had Maeve moved after their attack, finding her would have been nigh impossible.

"Do we walk right up or cut through the back again?"

Gavran chuckled. "Only thieves go in the back. She certainly won't trust us if we do that again."

They hadn't sought to steal from her before when they'd sliced their way into her home, but what they'd done hadn't been any better.

"The front then."

They passed the spot where, on their first trip to the town square, Gavran had bought bannocks and she'd given hers to the blind boy. The boy wasn't there now. Maybe if they made it out of this alive, she could find him and take him with her to Duntulm Castle if he had no family to care for him. Maybe Salome and Lord MacDonald would help her provide a home for all the children like him and Colin who would have trouble surviving in this world otherwise.

They stopped in front of Maeve's tent. The flap was up, and Maeve stood near the back, tipping a container of a powder into a smaller jar. Ceana stepped slightly to one side. Maybe if they weren't obviously a pair, Maeve wouldn't recognize them until it was too late.

"I've need of a spaewife's services," Gavran called. "Are you able to help me?"

"Aye. One moment."

Maeve capped her container and moved toward the tent opening.

Her skin was still as pale as lamb's wool, as if she too rarely saw the sun. As she turned, she opened her mouth, probably to invite Gavran in, but her expression shifted before the words came out. Her gaze shot toward the center of the square.

If she screamed, it wouldn't matter whether MacLeod guards

were close enough to hear her. One of the other men in the square would come.

Gavran shoved forward. He spun Maeve around, and his hand went over her mouth. Ceana darted in after them and dropped the tent flap. It might look suspicious to have it down this time of year, but Maeve's reaction to them hadn't left another option.

Sweat dampened the collar of Ceana's leine. With the tent closed, the temperature was blistering enough to melt off her skin. The air smelled of hot fabric and earthy herbs and smoke. "We're not here to hurt you."

Maeve rolled her eyes.

Ceana tugged at the strings holding the pouch to her waist. They tangled, and she dug her fingernail between the threads. The knot finally gave way. She dumped the glass shards out on Maeve's table. Some fragments were thumb sized, but most were no bigger than her fingernail, others no more than dust.

Flimsy proof that Salome had sent them, even to her eyes. "Lady MacDonald sent us back to you for help. She tried to send a bottle to prove to you that we'd come from her, but the fairy who cursed me attacked us on the way and it broke."

Even with only half her face showing under Gavran's hold, Maeve's raised eyebrows gave away exactly what she was thinking. That Ceana was a liar. That she must have some ulterior motive, even if it was only to extort something from Maeve without having to pay.

"I'm going to pull my hand away so you can answer." Gavran eased his hold, his hand still momentarily in place. "Please. We only want to talk."

He lowered his hand slowly, as if prepared to slap it back in place should Maeve try to cry out again.

Her eyes narrowed. "No *sgian* at my throat this time?"

The last time they were here, Ceana would have threatened to produce one if Maeve didn't cooperate. That woman was hardly one she'd recognize anymore. "No *sgian*. No matter what you say or do. We shouldn't have done that the first time. I was scared and desperate."

Maeve's features softened slightly. Her tight shoulders came down a fraction. "But not anymore?" Suspicion still laced her words.

Ceana bit back a laugh. Maybe more than ever. She had so much more to lose now than she would have thought possible the first time she'd stood in Maeve's tent. "Still. I've just learned that saving myself from the curse I'm under isn't worth it if I have to hurt others to do it."

"And if I want to walk out now?" Maeve took a step toward the tent flaps as if to emphasize her suggestion. "Call for MacLeod guards even. You won't stop me?"

Gavran tensed behind Maeve, but he didn't move. He watched Ceana. He would support her either way. At least he wouldn't have to stop her from hurting Maeve the way he had the first time.

Ceana stepped out of her path. "Then we'll let you go. But Salome sent us here because she trusts you."

Maeve twitched when Ceana used Salome's given name rather than her title.

The urge to extend her hands in supplication made her skin itch, but Maeve might easily see any move towards her as a threat. Ceana forced herself to stay still. "We need help. Will you listen at least?"

Maeve nodded, but she pulled the flap of the tent back open and stood in the middle of the opening. She motioned for Ceana and Gavran to sit.

The rapid beat of Ceana's pulse slowed. Maeve was willing to listen. Ceana took the closest chair. Gavran stepped around the small table to sit in the chair closer to the fire, despite the fact that beads of sweat already dripped down his temple.

As succinctly as she could, Ceana told Maeve everything that had happened to them since they first left Dunvegan for

Duntulm Castle. Halfway through, Maeve must have overcome her skepticism because she took the final chair at the table.

Ceana finished the story and let quiet descend on the tent. Outside, two men argued over the price of a pig. The normalcy of it compared to her own tale was laughable. Except that their situation wasn't actually funny, and the fairy could find them at any moment.

Maeve made a humming sound. "I know the story of the MacLeod fairy. I'm surprised the two of you don't. A puppet master acted it out for the children last market day."

Ceana's heart tugged slightly. She'd never watched a puppet show. Even as a little girl, her dadaidh hadn't wanted her wasting time on anything that couldn't bring in coins or barter. She'd tried only once to sneak away from him on market day to sit with the other children, and he'd slapped her so hard her teeth ached for days.

"My mamaidh didn't want us hearing any stories about the fae," Gavran's voice drew her away from the unpleasant memory and back into the present. "She was always worried the tales would make us too curious and get us into trouble."

Ceana drew her bottom lip between her teeth. Aye, Davina had been strict even before the cursed wishes changed history. But her own mamaidh had told her stories of the fae, at least the most common ones. Perhaps she hadn't considered the MacLeod fairy's story worth telling because it was a unique event. Though she had told Ceana about her in a sidelong fashion, about the woman on the road who'd warned her against marrying her dadaidh. Likely, her mamaidh hadn't made a connection between that fae woman and the MacLeod fairy. She'd have had no reason to.

Maeve glanced at the tent flaps, then shook her head gently, perhaps deciding that it'd look less suspicious to leave them open on such a hot day. The fabric of her tent wouldn't prevent the fairy from hearing them if she wanted anyway.

"I don't know her name. Her story doesn't give even a hint of one. But I'll tell it to you anyway."

Gavran nodded. "There might still be something in it that can lead us to her name."

His words warmed Ceana's insides as if he'd drawn her into his arms. The fairy could well find them before that, but if he was still brave enough to keep trying, how could she be anything less?

"It's one of the saddest stories among the fae." Maeve rose and shifted a pot of water over the hot coals in her fire. "Salome's story had a happy ending, but this one didn't."

Ceana clenched her jaw until she almost felt a pop. Perhaps the fairy got a small taste of the punishment she deserved then.

Maeve shot her a glance that was almost chiding, as if she suspected what Ceana was thinking. Gavran shifted in his chair. Ceana looked in his direction. His expression was sad.

Ah, she'd spoken aloud then without realizing it. "You heard what she did to me. To us."

Maeve placed three mugs on the table and spooned tea leaves into each of them. "Compassion shouldn't be reserved for those who deserve it. Otherwise, the Almighty erred when he forgave us."

Ceana's throat thickened. She still had a long way to go before she'd be the kind of person she wished to be. And Maeve having recently forgiven her, too.

"Some of the stories claim she was the daughter of the fairy king, and he allowed her to marry but only stay with her husband for a year less a day." Maeve returned the jar of leaves to the shelf over her trunk. She turned back to face them. "You know enough of the seelie and unseelie world now to know that can't be true."

Ceana swallowed, and her tight throat eased. Maeve showed grace in moving on. She was giving her a chance to be better. "Which means we have to approach the story with caution. There'll be false among the true."

"Aye." The water in Maeve's pot bubbled loudly enough to be

heard. She ladled it out into their cups. The soothing scent of chamomile filled the air. "I suspect she felt guilty for disobeying the Almighty's decree that seelie and unseelie weren't to marry or be given in marriage. She sought to return and face her punishment."

A repentant fairy was as close to the opposite of the fairy who'd forced the cursed wishes on them as imaginable. Ceana opened her mouth to voice the thought, then clamped her teeth together. She wouldn't speak rashly again. Look how she'd acted and felt right after the wishes took over. Many would judge her actions as wrong, and much of what she'd done had been. But no one could truly understand what it'd been like and why she'd made the choices she'd made unless they'd lived the same life. That didn't make her choices right. But it did mean she had to see the fairy as needing help, not censure. It's what she wanted for herself.

"But she'd already given birth to a child. A son." There was an ache in Maeve's voice. Had she lived life without one of her parents? "She made one request of her husband. That her son never be left to cry alone. That if he were to cry, someone would immediately go to him."

A rush of memory flooded over Ceana, and she closed her eyes. Of her mamaidh scooping up Colin when he'd cry for seemingly no reason as a bairn and a toddler. And her dadaidh saying her mamaidh's coddling would ruin the boy. That he needed to learn crying wouldn't get him anything. The same lesson he'd taught her.

"She's called the MacLeod fairy." Gavran blew gently on the liquid in his mug, not yet bringing it to his lips. "Her husband was a MacLeod?"

"Lord MacLeod, but one long enough past that no one can say which one. He was so grief-stricken at her leaving that he stayed by his son's cradle himself for weeks, not even leaving to eat or drink. His servants had to bring everything to him, and his family began to worry about the darkness under his eyes and his muscle dropping away."

Ceana's gaze drew to Gavran like a tide being pulled out to the sea. That raw feeling, where you were afraid to let yourself think too long about anything because everything would eventually lead back to the person you'd lost. Then as the edges healed over, the big aching hole still went with you everywhere.

She knew well the feeling that Lord MacLeod must have experienced after his wife left.

Gavran held her gaze tenderly. "She couldn't have been all bad. If he loved her that much."

She nodded, but the thought was large enough that it wedged going down. The fairy didn't make sense. She was so cruel. But then, grief—true grief, the kind that changed you—forced you to one side or the other. It hardened you. Or it softened you.

Maeve sipped her tea, though the steam must have burned a little. "Lord MacLeod's family was desperate to draw him out, so they invited friends to the castle to eat and drink and dance. Guests came from all across the isle. And still he refused to leave his son's side for fear he would cry and no one would hear him."

Ceana breathed in the calming aroma of her tea, earthy and soft, even though it was still too hot to drink. Lord MacLeod had clung to his son as the last piece of his wife. She could understand that part of his devotion, too. Hadn't she thought of finding Colin and protecting him for months, years? Not only for himself, but because now, he was the final link she had to her mamaidh.

"Did they succeed?" she asked.

Maeve dipped her head. "His sister brought her own bairn's nursemaid, promising that woman would stay by the child's side and sooth him if he cried. So he went to the feast. And he even allowed his family to convince him to dance one dance."

A darker edge entered Maeve's tone. Ceana squeezed her

knees together and wrapped her arms around her middle. This had to be where things turned.

"The nursemaid wasn't as reliable as he'd been led to believe. As soon as he was gone, she sneaked down to the kitchens for the servants' portion of the feast."

"Leaving the baby alone." Gavran's tight voice said he knew where this was headed as well.

"Aye." Maeve picked her mug up, then set it back down. "The boy kicked off his blankets and grew cold, wailing, but no one heard him over the music below. No one except his fairy mamaidh. She tore a swath of fabric from her gown and swaddled him in it and made him a promise that should he ever need her again, he or any of his descendants, all they needed to do was unfurl the fabric like a flag and wave it. She'd come. But only three times since everything must have its limits. She pressed that promise into his mind with a kiss so that he'd remember it as he grew."

Ceana held back a snort. The number three came up so often with the fae that at least a portion of the story must be true.

Four MacLeod guards strolled past the tent opening. Maeve rolled her eyes in their direction. "Some have exaggerated the tale to say a whole fairy army would appear to aid the MacLeods, but my mamaidh told it different. This was about a mamaidh's love for her child, not military might. And I trust her above those who'd have reason to exaggerate the flag's power."

The distinctive heavy clomp of the guards' hobnailed boots faded away. Ceana leaned forward, waiting for the ending.

Maeve kept her gaze on the tent's opening. "The fairy sought out her husband and saw him dancing with another while their bairn cried. She didn't destroy him the way she wanted to for the sake of their bairn, who would have been vulnerable to outside attack if his dadaidh were gone."

"But the betrayal she felt, she extended to all men." The words slipped out of Ceana before Maeve could finish.

If she'd had any doubt that the brollachan had rightly named the fairy who cursed them, she wouldn't have now. Her distrust of men, her anger towards them, her desire to protect women against what she saw as their inevitable betrayal made sense in light of her story. She believed her husband had forgotten about her and neglected their child after she'd been absent mere weeks.

"The worst of it is that she was wrong." Maeve turned her mugs around and around in her hands. "As my mamaidh told the story, she refused to believe the truth even once the humans involved spread word of what happened. She always thought it was a lie her husband made up to hide his own guilt."

The bleating of sheep crossing the square pierced the silence of the tent. Ceana turned the story over in her mind. They couldn't have long before the fairy realized they hadn't returned to Duntulm Castle. "Is there anything in there…?"

Gavran leaned back in his chair and crossed his arms over his chest. "I don't think that brings us any closer to a name. Least not as I can see." He shifted in Maeve's direction. "Do you know of anyone who might know details of the tale that you don't?"

Maeve rose and deposited her mug in a bucket of water. "My mamaidh and her mamaidh before her collected tales of the fae as protection. They knew every version of the stories ever told. That's the complete account of the MacLeod fairy and the fairy flag. And I don't think it brings you any closer to having a name for the fairy who cursed you than you were before."

CHAPTER 18

*C*eana couldn't breathe in the heavy, smoky air inside the tent any longer. She stood and moved to the entrance.

Behind her, Gavran questioned Maeve about the MacLeod fairy's story. *Was there no version in which Lord MacLeod called his wife by name? Were any names more common among women of MacLeod descent than others? Perhaps they'd carried on her name as a form of honor.*

Ceana looked off towards the water. The tower of Dunvegan castle rose above the stubbier buildings of the town proper. They couldn't go back to the seelie court with a guess. The risk of being wrong was too high. The court wouldn't give them a second chance. They had to know for sure.

That left only one option. The cooler evening breeze hit the back of her neck and sent a shiver down her spine. Gavran was going to call her an *eejit* as soon as he heard her idea, and he'd be right. She spun around to face them. "The only way to bring her name back to the seelie court is to have her give it to us."

Gavran jerked slightly, and his hand knocked his mug over. Tea spilled across Maeve's table. Maeve leaped to her feet, grabbed a cloth from her trunk, and mopped at the liquid running everywhere.

Gavran mumbled an apology. He pushed back his chair and moved out of Maeve's way, coming closer to where Ceana stood.

"Don't be an—"

Ceana raised her eyebrows. "An *eejit?*"

Gavran crushed his lips together. "Do you know of a better name to call someone who keeps throwing themselves off cliffs? The fairy isn't going to offer us her name. She nearly danced Eachann to his death to warn us off seeking it. And we're not strong enough to make her do any different. Every time we've met her face to face, we've come off the worse for it."

"Aye, I'm not arguing that." She needed him to listen, truly listen to her. She placed a hand on his arm.

He sucked in a quick breath, then let it out much more slowly, his shoulders relaxing. "Are you saying you have an idea for how we can change her mind?"

She rubbed her hand up and down the fabric covering his arm. The scratchiness was soothing in a way. Real in a world that had become much too much a nightmare. He'd follow her into whatever she suggested, nightmare or no. Not because she was guilting him into it or pressuring him in any way, but because he loved her. But was it fair to ask? This wouldn't be safe. What were the chances they could actually pull it off?

Gavran's fingers slid under her chin and brought her gaze up to his loch blue eyes. "You might as well tell me, love. The Almighty has kept us alive so far. Who's to say He won't do it again?"

She slid her hand over his, pressed it tighter and closed her eyes. They'd come this far. She couldn't let the fear of losing him stop her now. If they didn't succeed, she'd have lost him anyway. The fairy's words about how she could ultimately break the cursed wishes would always be there between them. Gavran would bring them up if he fell ill or grew injured or if there was ever a threat of them being separated. And she'd never be able to kill him. She'd taken one life, partly in defense and partly from selfishness, and she couldn't do it again, especially not to Gavran. Not even if he seemed moments from breathing his last. It wasn't her right to take a life.

She opened her eyes. His gaze was still steady on her face. From the corner of her eye, she glimpsed Maeve watching them silently, the damp cloth clutched in her hands.

Ceana breathed out, and it sounded loud in her ears. "However misguided, her actions in the story were based on love. I think the fairy flag would still be valuable to her. She wants it left with the MacLeods, her descendants. What if we stole it and threatened to destroy it?"

Gavran's fingers twitched against her cheek. "You think she'll trade her name for the flag?"

Ceana nodded. And once the deal was struck, the fairy wouldn't be able to go back on it. Their interactions with the unseelie fae, who would have loved to violate their bargains, had proved that.

She turned towards Maeve. Gavran dropped his hand but stayed beside her.

"What do you think?" she asked. "Based on all you know, does it have a chance of succeeding?"

Maeve dropped the soaked cloth into the same bucket of water where she'd deposited her mug earlier. "A chance, aye. But you'd have to get into Dunvegan castle first, and that wouldn't even be your biggest challenge. You need MacLeod blood to touch the fairy flag. Anyone without MacLeod blood who touches the flag goes mad."

CHAPTER 19

*T*he slightly macabre desire to laugh bubbled up in Ceana's chest again. Maybe it wouldn't matter if she touched the MacLeod flag. Maybe everything that happened had taken her off her head already. Laughing certainly wasn't a healthy reaction to Maeve's announcement.

"Anyone who doesn't carry MacLeod blood goes mad if they touch the flag," Gavran repeated as if he wasn't sure he'd heard her correctly.

"So the stories go." Maeve motioned them back to her table.

Ceana took a step and swayed on her feet. Perhaps Maeve was wise to insist upon sitting. Her body seemed to think this last pronouncement was one blow beyond what she could bear.

She tottered back to the table. At least soon she'd be able to rest, one way or the other, either because the curse was lifted or because she'd gone to be with the Lord where she'd have eternal peace. She just had to keep her wits about her a little longer.

Gavran helped her into her seat and then took his own.

Maeve sat last. "A few have tried over the years to steal a scrap of the fairy flag. They wanted their own share of the blessing and were foolish enough to believe they could steal it."

Ceana forced her spine to straighten rather than slumping in the chair. A slumped person was a defeated person, and she wasn't done yet. "And what happened to them? How do you know they went mad?"

Maeve's gaze flickered in the direction of Dunvegan. "They threw themselves off the top of Dunvegan tower."

Certainly not the outcome she wanted. The memory of looking down into the dark of the deep ditch surrounding Duntulm Castle flitted across her mind. She'd been less ready to plummet to her death then than she'd thought, and she certainly had more to live for now. "What if we don't touch it with our skin? We could wrap something around our hands."

Maeve shrugged. "I don't know if it's ever been tried before."

Ceana bit her lip and looked down at the table. She traced the wood grain with her pinky finger. Following it helped her slide everything in her mind into place. "There are two of us. One could take the flag with covered hands. The other would be there to stop them if the stories about the protection and what it does to any non-MacLeod are true."

"And have one of us be madder than a rabid fox for the rest of our lives?" Gavran's tone said *absolutely not*.

Ceana gave up on tracing the pattern. "The seelie court can lift the madness the same as they can the cursed wishes. Surely the fairy shouldn't have put that sort of protection onto an object left in human hands to begin with."

"I'm sure she shouldn't have," Maeve said softly, as if she needed to speak the truth but didn't want to encourage them in something that would be akin to suicide.

Gavran crossed his arms, his expression sharp-edged as chiseled rock. "And I suppose you expect me to allow you to be the one to take the risk of touching the fae-blasted flag."

Calm had fallen over her, the same way the morning after a storm felt. This had to be done. "Aye, I'll be the one nabbing the flag. If you were to go off your head, I'm not strong enough to keep you from throwing yourself from the top of the walls. Or to stop you from getting too far from me."

Gavran lowered his arms and let his hands drop to the table. He fisted and unfisted them. "Do you have any idea what it will do to me if your body's still here, but I lose you?"

She did. She'd faced him that first day she'd regained consciousness in his family's cottage, and he'd seen only a stranger. She'd had to bind him when the nuckalevee venom turned her into the enemy in his mind.

And she knew it was still better than what would happen to her if he went mad or threw himself off the castle walls, and she had to live under the cursed wishes until the end of her days. "I won't survive the wishes again. My mind will break anyway, along with my spirit. I have to be the one to take the risk."

Gavran lowered his face into his hands. His silence spoke his agreement even though he couldn't seem to manage the words.

Outside, the sky was turning from blue to red as the sun disappeared. How much longer could they hope to have before the fairy found them again? Morning perhaps. If the Almighty smiled on them.

Maeve went to a shelf near the fire and brought back a round loaf of bread with even slits on the top and a chunk of cheese. "You still have to get into Dunvegan before you can even hope to try grabbing the fairy flag. I might have an idea on how to do it. If you're willing to take the risk."

CHAPTER 20

*C*eana tried to swallow down the bannock that Gavran had purchased for her with the coins Maeve left for them. The oat cake was hot and fresh and should have crumbled deliciously in her mouth. Instead she might as well have tried to choke down a mouthful of leaves.

Gavran smiled at her, but the edges of his lips were tight. "It shouldn't be much longer now. The town's usually swarming with guards first thing in the morn."

Ceana gave up on the bannock and glanced around. They'd gone over Maeve's idea last night until the words stopped making sense. Her plan had been the only way to get into Dunvegan Castle. That didn't mean she felt good about it. There were so many ways it could go wrong, and they could both end up rotting in a forgotten cell.

Maeve's colorful shawl flashed at the edge of the square where she stood with three MacLeod guards. Finally.

Ceana dropped her gaze, though nothing she did now would make any difference. The accusation had been made. The pieces were in place.

The guards drew close.

"You there," called the one who was so tall and thin that he looked as though he'd been squashed out underneath a boulder. "Stay where you are."

Don't run. She had to stay still even though every instinct inside screamed at her to flee. They wanted to be brought in for questioning. They didn't want to do anything to actually appear guilty.

The burliest of the guards clamped a hand around Gavran's arm, and the oldest one, whose face had more wrinkles than a prune, took her by the wrist.

The tall guard laid a hand on the pommel of his sword. "We're taking you to the castle on the suspicion that you're MacDonald spies."

Don't fight them. She repeated Maeve's instructions over and over in her head. Let *Gavran do the talking.*

"We returned only last night from MacDonald land, but we're no spies." Somehow Gavran managed to infuse the perfect balance of confusion and fear into his words. "I've spent all my younger years on MacLeod land."

The tall guard's fingers tightened on the grip of his sword. "And what were you doing on MacDonald lands at all if you're loyal to the MacLeods?"

Ceana's heart beat so fast and hard that the thrum became a sustained buzz in her ears. Almighty save them from destroying the fragile peace that currently existed between the MacDonalds and the MacLeods. The line they were walking was so fine as to be nearly invisible.

But their choices had been limited. Only servants and requested deliveries were allowed entrance into the castle. With the fairy sure to soon realize what they'd done, they didn't have time to try to enter by either of those means. And a more minor crime like stealing would have seen them immediately punished by the guards rather than brought to the castle.

Gavran hesitated the perfect amount of time before answering. She never would have been able to read the guards and find the balance the way he did. "I had the offer of an apprenticeship."

The guards should now be wondering why he couldn't have found an apprenticeship on MacLeod lands. It didn't prove their guilt. It didn't clear them either. It made sure the guards would need to bring them before Lord MacLeod for a decision.

And in the meantime, Ceana could only pray that the story they'd come up with about her Uncail Lyall the physician offering Gavran a place with him would be enough to save their necks if they weren't able to get to the flag. Nothing would spare them if they were caught stealing it.

The burly guard pushed Gavran ahead of him, keeping his grip on Gavran's upper arm as he did. "You'll need to tell your story to Lord MacLeod and hope he believes you then."

The guards escorted them through the streets and down to the docks. The townspeople they passed looked away as if afraid to be associated with them by even so much as a glance. Not that she could blame them. Anyone who was being escorted by MacLeod guards the way they were might as well have been branded across the forehead with the word *trouble*.

As they got closer to the water, a red-billed oystercatcher took flight from where it'd been wading in the shallows, hunting for a meal.

The small rowboat the guards must have taken from the castle to the shore rocked back and forth in the water.

Ceana's breath threatened to turn solid and choke her. Why hadn't she considered what going to Dunvegan Castle would mean? Of course they'd have to go out on the water. The castle was completely surrounded by water. There was no land access.

The last time she'd been out on water had been the night the fairy had saved her and Gavran from drowning only to doom them to a worse fate. She couldn't go away from land again, not with the fairy after them. If she caught them on the water, there'd be no escape. No way to run. And who knew what the fairy would decide to do this time.

Her feet weighed heavier than the rocks lining the shore, and she stumbled. Her body backed up before she could stop herself. The guard holding her tightened his grip. His fingers dug into her flesh, pinching, and she flinched.

The guard yanked her roughly forward. Her feet splashed into the water, cold against the rest of her that seemed to be burning. Black flickered around the edges of her vision.

"She's afraid of the water." Gavran's voice from behind her. "She's not trying to run."

Her palms hit the rough wood of the bottom of the row boat, a splinter finding its way under her skin. How had she gotten into the boat? She had to get out. Now.

Arms wrapped around her, along with Gavran's voice.

"Breathe, love. Breathe." He pressed her face into his chest, blocking her sight of the loch.

She sucked in air. Only a little at first, then more. Gavran's familiar smell along with the brine and algae scents of the sea.

Not so different from when he'd wrapped an arm around her and done his best to swim them to shore. The water had been so cold her hands and feet stopped hurting after a while and all she's wanted to do was sleep. They'd been arguing about him letting her drown, saving himself.

Then the fairy came.

She shivered, unable to keep her body still. The words and images rolled over and over in her head until she wanted to scream.

"We're here." Gavran peeled her back enough that sunlight hit her eyes through her eyelids. "We made it."

She forced her eyes open. He'd managed to turn her so, when she did, the slab of basalt where Dunvegan Castle sat towered above them, at least as high as five of her family's cottages stacked atop each other. A small patch of dry land, so green as to feel almost indecent, nestled up to the side of the row boat. She scrambled for it and dropped out of the boat on her hands and knees. The ground was soggy but solid.

"I thought he was making stories," one of the guards said, his words mumbled, "but she looks like she's going to kiss that scrubby grass."

He let out an oof, as if the second guard had elbowed him. "Let's get them inside and be done with it."

Ceana buried her fingers in the grass beneath her for a moment more. Her head cleared slowly. The bump and bubble of water cascading down the becks that drew lines down the basalt plug replaced the thrumming of her own heartbeat in her ears.

She rose slowly to her feet. The water still lurked at the edge of her vision, but two otters played in it, as if to try to show her there wasn't a threat. Even if she hadn't been avoiding a crazed fairy, she doubted she would have agreed with them. Open water would always come with memories she couldn't shake.

The guard with the weather-worn face pointed towards the steps carved into the steep rock. "You first."

He followed behind her. The steps were narrow enough that she didn't dare look back for fear of losing her balance, but it seemed like a safe guess that Gavran followed her guard and the burly guard brought up the rear.

Her next step slipped on the rock made slick by sea spray. She righted herself and dragged a hand along the rockward side of the steps for the rest of the climb. She hadn't come this far to do the fairy's job for her by plummeting to her death before she even reached Dunvegan Castle.

She'd have to make sure she included placing them safely back in the town of Dunvegan as part of their deal with the fairy upon stealing the fairy flag. She never had learned to swim, and "borrowing" a boat to return to the mainland without being caught seemed unlikely.

The stairs ended at a small landing two-thirds of the way up at a small iron-barred doorway. Two guards stood inside.

Her guard moved her to the side and spoke in low tones to the men behind the bars. She could catch only a few words... *Spies. Interrogate.*

A cold line trailed over her skin. Hopefully the words she'd missed had been *possible* and to *find out the truth*.

The guards unlocked the gate, and Ceana's guard preceeded her this time. She followed along behind him. As soon as they were past the entrance, there wasn't room for her to do anything else. If she stuck her elbows out on both sides, she would have bumped one, if not both, against the walls. The air was cold as fall, and the narrow tunnel held onto the lantern's smoke, making the air thick and sharp when she would have otherwise expected damp and musty.

Lanterns provided barely enough light for her to see every time they passed a guard standing stock still in one of the alcoves that appeared to have been carved out for those very purposes. Dunvegan was defensive in a way Duntulm wasn't.

Just when she thought she might never emerge from the twisting passages, she stepped out into the courtyard, the sun so bright it hurt. Gulls swooped in the air above her, and she gulped in a lungful of fresh air ripe with the warm smells of horse sweat and sheep dung alongside the hint of the sea that still hung over everything.

The guards didn't let them hesitate. They urged them in the direction of the tower. Somehow, without any signal from their guards that she could see, more joined them, until the two had become four.

Her stomach muscles seized uncomfortably. This might very well have been her worst and most reckless idea. At least the unseelie had been predictable in some sense. She'd known what they would want. She could anticipate the games they'd try to play. But humans had no type she could match them against.

Each was uniquely formed. The rumors that lay beneath the basis of her knowledge of Lord MacLeod were almost sketchier than the picture Salome had been able to draw them of the nuckalevee or the banshee or the brollachan.

The guards escorted them through the Great Hall, its fire only a smoulder and its large tables empty of food and people at this time of day. Above the hearth hung the MacLeod motto—HOLD FAST—etched into a polished wooden plaque and mounted beneath a bull's head, its sightless eyes staring out into the room. Bile burned Ceana's throat, and she averted her gaze.

Killing to eat, she understood. She'd done it herself. But turning the dead into trophies spoke to a hardness of heart towards His creatures that the Almighty surely never intended.

They approached the end of the hall where the high table for the lord and his lady and honored guests stood at a right angle to all the others.

Ceana's footsteps faltered, and she slowed. Right above the largest chair, the one with the ornately carved back, hung a square of slightly faded green fabric in an oak frame. Delicately embroidered gold crosses and red rowen berries adorned the fabric's surface. It took no imagination at all to see it as part of a lady's gown from the past. The fairy might have even spent her time awaiting her son's birth embellishing the fabric herself, perhaps using whatever magic she had to stitch protection into it for herself, not dreaming at the time that she'd one day leave it as a legacy for her child.

Heavy hands shoved into her back. "Keep moving."

Ceana's hands tingled with the desire to grab the flag and race to the fire. But if she made a move for it now, an overzealous guard could easily run her through before she'd made it halfway.

She buried her hands in the apron Maeve had loaned her instead. When the time came, she'd take it off and use it to protect her hands from the touch of the fairy flag. But now wasn't that moment.

She glanced at Gavran. He lifted his chin the slightest fraction. He'd seen it too.

At least they hadn't had to search the castle. She should have guessed. Lord MacLeod's pride was legendary. Where else would he keep the flag that declared him to have powerful fae blood running through his veins? He'd want anyone who entered his home to see it there and wonder if he also had abilities they couldn't imagine. He'd want them to think carefully before crossing him.

Not an enemy she'd have chosen for herself, but once this was over, they'd flee back to MacDonald land. They'd have to hide until Lord MacDonald smoothed over whatever trouble they caused. Assuming he could.

They wouldn't give their true names. They'd make sure this couldn't come back on Gavran's family.

They simply had to bide their time, and wait for their chance to come back for the flag. The guards would place them somewhere to wait for Lord MacLeod to be ready to speak to them. Hopefully they wouldn't be considered dangerous enough to need more than a single guard—two at most—while within the walls of the castle. The *sgians* Maeve helped her strap to her legs weren't much, nor were the lockpicking implements sewed into a pocket Maeve added on the inside of her dress bodice, but they'd give them a chance of escaping once the guards settled them and relaxed somewhat.

She kept walking, not looking back at the flag again. At the far end of the Hall, they entered another dark corridor.

Blessedly shorter this time at least.

It opened into a cave-like, round room, empty except for an iron-grille inlaid into the floor.

The guards who'd joined them during their trek across the courtyard lifted the grate, grunting with the weight of it.

Ceana's mouth dried out so much that her tongue thickened. They were going to place them in a pit dungeon? She'd been expecting a cell like they'd experienced at Duntulm Castle at worst and a bare room at best. Those were what they'd prepared for. A pit dungeon was where you placed the worst criminals, ones you wanted to allow to starve while smelling the feasts prepared in the nearby kitchens and consumed in the Great Hall.

Gavran straightened up and frowned. "The lord hasn't determined our guilt yet."

The younger guard holding the grille snickered.

"Hurry it up," the older of the two said, sounding out of breath. "This thing weighs as much as the two of you put together."

The burly guard who'd brought them from town flipped a rude gesture in his direction. He gathered a rope tied off to a loop in the floor. He tossed it to Gavran. "Climb down."

Her gaze met Gavran's. He forced a tiny smile, and she returned it. They had to obey. They'd have to figure out their next step once they were inside. Pit dungeons were usually built deep enough that even two tall men, one standing on the other's shoulders, couldn't reach the iron grille. And even if they'd been able to reach it, it was clearly heavy enough that it took two men, not one, and certainly not someone as small as her to lift.

Maybe they'd have to wait until Lord MacLeod called for them. They'd have to plan what to say to keep from actually being charged as spies. But at least the fairy wouldn't be able to get at them with the iron grille covering the only way in or out.

Gavran turned and used the rope to half walk, half hop down into the depths of the pit.

She reached for the rope to follow him.

The weathered guard jerked her back. "Not you. Lord MacLeod will see you first."

The guards dropped the iron grille down over Gavran's prison with a clang.

CHAPTER 21

*C*eana's breath stumbled in and out of her lungs, catching and hitching. They weren't supposed to separate them. She and Gavran were supposed to stay together. What if the guards took her too far away from him and the cursed wishes took over again? Not only wouldn't she get the flag, but—

She cut off her own thoughts, forcing her mind away, forcing it onto the sound of the guards' boots on the stones, onto the smell of old sweat from the one on the right and the turnips the one on the left had recently eaten. Onto anything to keep her mind from spiralling to a place where she couldn't control it and her body shut down.

Should she fight them? But even if she did, and she could race back to Gavran, she couldn't possibly lift the iron grille herself, not when it'd taken two men to do it.

Fighting them was a fool's dream anyway. She'd never be able to break free from four armed men, not with how two walked in front of her and two behind. They had no reason not to kill her if she tried to flee. What did they care if she wasn't a spy? She was nothing to them or to Lord MacLeod.

She slowed her steps as much as the guards would allow.

She was nothing to them. Nothing to Lord MacLeod.

But she was something to the fairy. For whatever reason, the fairy was determined to "help" her—or, at least, what she saw as helping. Gavran had been convinced she meant well even if she was blind to the fact that how she went about it was cruel.

So could she use that? She'd been in danger before. Since the fairy had pulled her and Gavran from the loch the night they almost drowned, the fairy had never come to her aid, regardless of what happened to her. Not when she was starving. Not when she was beaten. Not when an unseelie was trying to kill her.

Physical peril must be seen by the fairy as part of her lesson.

One of the guards behind her shoved her hard in the back with two knuckles. "Stop dragging yer feet. It won't help yer case none to make his lordship wait on you."

She made note of the turn they took. At the end of the hall, stairs rose upward. Lord MacLeod must be in one of the tower rooms. If they took her up the tower, the distance would no doubt be far enough that the blessing side and the curse side of the wishes stopped canceling each other out. She'd be under the sway of the wishes again. How far had she already gone from Gavran? Was it already too late?

She sucked in a sharp breath. From Gavran. That was it.

The fairy wanted something very specific from her. If she offered it, surely the fairy would appear to aid her in carrying it out.

"I've learned my lesson," she said softly, "but I can't prove it while I'm held captive."

The guard behind her jabbed his knuckles into her back again, hard enough that it would surely leave a bruise. "What're you babbling about?"

The youngest of the guards, one whose face was only growing downy fuzz, turned back and scowled. "Leave her be. She's more likely not right in the head than a spy."

A lump of gratitude filled her throat. He might not be able to show her full kindness given the situation, but his willingness to stand up to guards much his senior still showed some character. Not that it would help her at all.

Nor did it seem like the fairy was coming.

The guard behind her poked her again. She could almost feel his smirk in the action.

She'd try one more time. The fairy wasn't omnipresent. Maybe she hadn't heard her. "I've learned my lesson." She shouted it this time. It certainly couldn't cause any harm if the guards thought she wasn't all there in the head. "I need my freedom to prove it."

"If she keeps on like that in front of Lord MacLeod," the other front guard said, "we're the ones who'll have to pay for wasting his time."

What other hope did she have than to keep trying. "I've learned my—"

A hard blow landed on the back of her head. She bit the inside of her cheek, and the metallic tang on blood coated her tongue. Her ears buzzed.

She stumbled sideways slightly. One of the guards in front—the young one—stuck out an arm. She grabbed it and righted herself. Her balance steadied.

A scream split the air behind her, then a clang and a thud. The younger guard froze. The guard next to him jerked back a step, tugging at his sword as if he couldn't remember how to draw it. Or couldn't draw it.

Ceana spun around as quickly as she dared with her head still pounding.

The fairy stood, a sword that must have belonged to one of the guards who'd been trailing her in her hand. Blood coated its blade, and the guard who'd presumably owned it lay at her feet, his palms braced against his stomach. The other guard slumped against the far wall, his neck at an unnatural angle.

Bile burned Ceana's throat. This wasn't what she'd intended.

She should have thought through the consequences of calling on the fairy for help. Those deaths—the guard holding his stomach was surely losing too much blood to survive—were at least partly on her for her rashness.

The fairy flicked her wrist, and the sword she'd been holding flew past Ceana. A squishy, gurgling noise followed.

She didn't dare look back. Didn't dare see what that sword had done and to which of the guards it'd done it.

The fairy stalked towards her, then past. She didn't glance in Ceana's direction.

Run, a soft voice whispered in Ceana's head.

And this time, instead of the times before, she listened. Because if she couldn't reach the fairy flag hanging in the Great Hall before the fairy finished with the final guard and came after her, all their deaths would be in vain.

CHAPTER 22

Ceana turned the corner. Two guards running towards the sounds of the fairy's slaughter nearly collided with her. She swerved to the side and bounced off the wall. They didn't even look. They turned the corner and were gone.

Would the fairy kill them too? This wasn't how it was supposed to go. The fairy should have... What had she thought the fairy would do? She hadn't even considered it. She should have. She knew what the fairy was capable of. She'd only been thinking about herself. And now there was nothing she could do to change it.

Shouts were flowing from other parts of the castle. Someone had raised the alarm.

She ran faster and skidded into the small chamber where Gavran huddled in the pit dungeon. Dirt and pebbles kicked up by her feet rattled down into the hole, probably pelting Gavran's head and shoulders.

No time for her to explain. She took the short passage at the other side and burst out into the Great Hall.

She stopped so suddenly that she nearly lost her balance again and fell. Her vision spun slightly. Six guards stood between her and the fireplace where she'd planned to hold the fairy flag hostage. Based on their hand gestures and raised voices, they were clearly making plans for how to split up to search the castle for the invaders they assumed were inside.

An unearthly screech ricocheted through the castle walls as if they were parchment instead of stone. The fairy had realized she'd been double-crossed. It'd be mere moments before she was on top of her. Maybe she'd kill her in her rage like she'd killed the guards.

She needed fire that she could keep with her. She darted back to the chamber with the pit dungeon and tore the torch from its holder on the wall.

Slowing her pace only enough to make sure she didn't set herself ablaze, she jogged back to the Great Hall and straight for the fairy flag. She reached a hand behind her to untie the apron. She'd planned to have both hands for this. The knot refused to give.

The air shimmered next to her, and then the fairy was there. Her gaze landed on Ceana, her eyes as hard and green and shimmering as emeralds.

"You lied to me." The words had a soft hiss to them, the way an adder might sound as it bared its fangs.

Chaos seemed to erupt behind her, in the direction where the guards had been congregating next to the fire. A yell. The zing of metal against leather as weapons came free. Heavy footfalls.

The fairy moved so fast she was a blur. Standing in front of Ceana one second, then behind her, then dragging a guard away. The guards broke apart, some coming for Ceana, some racing in the direction the fairy had gone.

Before she could clear her head enough to think straight or move, the fairy was back. But instead of the guard she'd taken, she held Gavran around the throat. Only his toes touched the floor, and his face was blotchy red.

She must have used the guard somehow to remove the iron grille from the pit dungeon since she wouldn't have been able to touch the iron herself. If she'd left the poor man alive, he might be lying in agony with both shoulders dislocated from the weight of lifting it himself.

Clatter from the direction of the passage to the pit dungeon. At least some of the guards who'd gone that way were returning.

The fairy lifted Gavran half a finger's width, just enough so his feet dangled, his toes reaching for purchase. He made a gagging noise.

"Last chance." The fairy's voice was calm and firm. "You kill him quickly. Or I will make him suffer while you watch the life slowly leech from his body."

Ceana forced herself to keep her gaze on the fairy's face rather than shifting to where the fairy flag hung. She was so close. If she sprang for it, she might be able to grab it.

A thick arm wrapped around her waist. "This way, miss. Come with me."

The guard's words were so different from the fairy's. Calm, but with an underlying note of panic. He didn't know why she was there. He must have come from the passage leading to the pit dungeon and spotted her standing, seemingly frozen in terror, near a clearly supernatural being who was strangling someone. Given the comparison, he would never guess the role she'd played in all of it. Any other time, she'd admire his bravery, placing himself in danger to save her.

But she couldn't leave. She squirmed against him. "Let me go."

His hold tightened, and he backed up a step, clearly intending to take her out of harm's way whether she wanted it or not.

She went limp in his hold, making sure he had to deal with all her weight on him, making it harder for him. She brought the torch closer to her and pointed the flame toward the floor.

"Let me go." She made sure to speak loudly and clearly. "Let me go, or I'll send us both up in flames."

The guard hesitated for one breath, two, as if he wasn't sure whether she'd lost her senses from the fear. Then he let her go.

She couldn't hesitate. She tightened her grip on the torch and lunged for the fairy flag.

CHAPTER 23

Ceana's fingers closed around the middle of the fairy flag, and she yanked. The cloth tore from its framing. The frame swayed on the wall, then plunged to the floor. The wood cracked.

She refused to look to see how much of the flag she might have left behind. It didn't matter. She'd gotten most of it, even if the edges were more ragged now than they might have originally been.

More guards spilled into the room every minute. She backed up so that another guard couldn't sneak up on her from behind.

She met the fairy's gaze. She'd lowered Gavran enough that his toes were on the floor again, and he was sucking in big, rasping breaths. The fairy's expression was slightly blank, as if Ceana had surprised her for the first time since the night of the wishes when she'd taken the cursed-side for herself and had given the blessing-side to Gavran.

Ceana brought the fairy flag close to the torch's flame. The fairy flag was old enough that all it would likely take to turn it to ash was a single spark. The fairy shot out her free hand even though she was much too far from Ceana to stop her.

"I want to make a deal." Ceana worked hard to keep her focus on the fairy rather than on Gavran. She had to keep a level head and listen closely to everything the fairy said. She had to choose her words as carefully. There was no room for error this time.

"For his life?" The fairy didn't lower herself enough to curl her lip, but it was in her tone. Ceana's willingness to sacrifice herself for Gavran repeatedly disgusting her. "Again?"

Ceana gave herself a breath. She could bargain for the fairy to lift the curse from them, as well as spare Gavran. The fairy flag seemed to mean enough to her that she might do it. But what were the chances that she could lay out terms in enough detail not to leave the fairy a loophole to still hurt them or trick them? At least if they took her name back to the seelie court, Eliezer would be there to advocate for them. And the seelie court didn't actively want to hurt them. They wouldn't be looking for a double cross. Plus, if she made a deal to lift the cursed wishes, it didn't protect anyone else from the fairy.

She needed to stick to their plan.

"Aye, for his life, but also for your name. Your true name. Your personal name. The one the Almighty gave you when he created you."

Two guards tried to creep up behind the fairy. She swept a hand backward, brushing against her skirt the way a mortal woman might brush off a spider. The guards toppled and skidded across the stone floor, their chainmail scraping and jangling.

"What could you possibly want my name for?" The fairy spoke quietly enough that she could have meant it only for herself. She looked between Ceana and Gavran. "You managed to contact the seelie court somehow, didn't you? And they promised to remove my gift in exchange for knowing who gave it to you."

There was something in her voice. Not quite resignation. Something akin to it, though. Like she might be glad for her decades and decades of vengeance to finally be brought to an end. Like she was exhausted in the way that only an immortal who'd dedicated their lifetime to things that could never satisfy could be.

The fairy brought Gavran down enough that the soles of his feet touched the ground, though she didn't remove her hand from his throat. "If you can tell me why I bestowed your gift, then I will give you my name—the one bestowed upon me by the Lord God Almighty at the moment of my creation that is my essence and nature."

So she wouldn't do it for the sake of preserving the flag alone. Perhaps that had been too much to hope for. The child she'd given the flag to was long dead, and passing over her name held consequences for the rest of her existence.

They had Maeve's story of what had happened to the fairy. Perhaps the fairy didn't realize they knew it. They might have been going for the fairy flag simply because they'd heard it would summon the aid of the fae, rather than because they knew it mattered to this fairy in particular. If so, then Ceana had the advantage here.

She shifted her gaze the tiniest bit so Gavran's face wavered at the edge of her vision. Except the fairy hadn't mentioned the other part of Ceana's original request. This would not be straightforward. If Ceana wasn't careful, she could strike this deal only to have the fairy kill Gavran in front of her.

"You'll give us your name and allow us both"—she motioned between herself and Gavran—"safe passage to bring it to the seelie court. You'll place us back in the streets of Dunvegan yourself. You won't do anything to harm us or stop us or delay us."

The fairy's lips turned up at the edges. "In turn, you will return what I value to me." She pointed a single finger at the fairy flag. "And I will not wait forever. You cannot delay either. Three guesses. Made this day."

If she never dealt with multiples of three again, she would praise the Lord for her blessings. "Our deal is struck."

The fairy swirled her hand. The Great Hall blurred around Ceana. Her stomach leapt, then plunged.

Then she was swaying, staring out through an embrasure atop a parapet wall and across blue-green water. A peninsula covered over with trees reached fingers out into the water on her left, and a hazy landmass stretched across the horizon in the distance. A breeze that was almost cool tugged at her clothes.

She tottered back a step and glanced around her.

The fairy perched atop the battlement, seated as comfortably as if it'd been the king's throne. On the merlon next to hers, Gavran balanced in a standing position, still as if he'd been frozen in ice other than for his wide eyes darting in all directions.

Her heart shouldn't have been able to beat any faster without killing her, and yet it had—going from distinct thuds to a hard flutter within her chest. Somehow the fairy had transported them to the top of Dunvegan tower.

"I wanted privacy for our contest." The fairy smiled at her, then tilted her head back to look at Gavran. "And if you fail, I'll have the pleasure of tossing him off."

CHAPTER 24

*C*eana let the torch drop to her feet and roll away. It'd gone out in their rapid trip anyway. Not that she needed it. Their deal was struck, and the fairy must abide by the terms.

She let her gaze stray back to Gavran's precarious position. No doubt the fairy had placed him there to unsettle her, fog her thinking.

And perhaps it should have. Perhaps with someone else it would have. But she'd been through too much. Setting him up there, threatening his life, only made her more determined to stay calm and win this game. Seeing him there, silhouetted against the clouds, brought every memory of their past together and every hope she had for the future crashing together in her mind.

She sent up a silent prayer for peace and for wisdom.

She'd never be able to match the fairy's strength and power, but it was human beings who'd been created in God's image. She'd out-thought the fairy once, the night they'd first met and she'd taken the curse the fairy intended for Gavran on herself. She could do it again.

She had to do it again.

"What's your first guess, my dear child?" The fairy looked significantly up at the sun above them. The way she phrased the question made it sound as if she were confident Ceana would either run out of guesses or time before discovering her secret.

Ceana balled one end of the fairy flag in her fist. The fabric was softer than she would have imagined when she'd first seen it hanging on the wall.

"You were married to a former Lord MacLeod. But you were seelie, and you knew you couldn't stay with him. When you decided to leave, you made only one request of him, and he betrayed you."

Whether he had or not didn't seem to be the point. The fairy had believed her husband had, and that had colored everything she'd done since.

The fairy's smile hardened, as if it were made of stone rather than flesh.

Ceana bit down hard on her lower lip. The fairy was too still. If she'd guessed right, shouldn't there have been a reaction from her? Anger, most likely. Though the fairy's lack of reaction did reveal something. What had happened to her still rubbed raw. Ceana's guess might not have been correct, but the answer lay somewhere inside, like an acorn in its shell.

"That's a part of my history, true. It doesn't, however, fulfill your part of our bargain. You were to tell me why I bestowed your gift, not how I found out that all men, no matter what they say, will one day betray you." She lifted her hand, and Gavran took a half step back toward the edge of the merlon and the water below. "Two guesses remain to you."

Ceana rubbed her teeth back and forth over her bottom lip until the pain made her stop. Had the fairy's reply been a trick to send her down the wrong path? Or had hearing her own history retold so bluntly unsettled her enough that she'd made a mistake and given Ceana the clue she'd need to solve this.

There was only one way to find out, but if she was wrong, she'd be down to her final guess.

She met Gavran's gaze. He managed to move his head enough to give her the tiniest nod. It felt like him saying he trusted her, believed in her, loved her.

She filled her lungs to capacity and let the air out. The fairy had seemed to be saying that she hadn't been specific enough in her answer.

The night they'd met, the fairy had said she'd warned her mamaidh not to marry her dadaidh. And she and Gavran had wondered if she'd been going through the years "helping" other women the way she'd helped Ceana.

"You gave me my gift"—the word lodged in her throat, and she had to force it out—"because you want to protect other women from being deceived and betrayed. My gift was supposed to free me from the need to depend on men."

The fairy's eyes softened at the edges. She slid from her seat and glided toward Ceana.

The instinct to flee swelled inside her. She concentrated on staying still. Did the fairy's approach mean she'd guessed correctly or not? Her answer made sense. It had to be right.

The fairy cupped Ceana's cheek. The touch was almost... loving. Her mamaidh used to caress her face in the same way when Ceana was little.

A tiny, tight knot coiled in Ceana's chest. There was no way this was a defeated fairy. This was all wrong.

"You finally see why I had to do what I did." The fairy stroked her thumb along Ceana's cheekbone, then lowered her hand. "I had to try to spare you the heartache that I experienced. You loved him too much. You would have done almost anything for him. And he would have only used you, then tossed you aside when you were no longer useful."

Her tone sharpened at the end.

Wrong, wrong, wrong. The word thrummed in her head. All

wrong. Had she left the fairy some way to still hurt Gavran if she guessed correctly? Nay, she'd included that she and Gavran both had to be allowed to return to the seelie court safely. "But Gavran hasn't done any of that. He could have many times." Dare she say it? It seemed like the fairy needed to hear someone say it. Allowing her to go on like this if Ceana failed and the fairy wasn't brought to justice before the seelie court was unthinkable. "Your husband didn't betray you either. Not if any of the many stories about what happened are true. He loved you so much he lost his will to go on after you left. His one mistake was placing his trust in the woman who was supposed to care for your son while he tried to ease his family's worries."

The fairy hissed in a breath. "I've heard those lies. Heard them told over and over for years. But I know the truth because I've also watched for centuries how men have taken advantage of women. How women were nothing more than property. Things to be used. It was not supposed to be that way in the Almighty's plan. The Almighty created women in his own image alongside men, equal in value. Once I felt the pain of it, how could I be expected to stand by and continue to allow it to happen to others?"

Gavran had been right about what was driving the fairy, then. She was fighting for the way things should be, but she was doing it in a way that was equally wrong.

Ceana edged toward Gavran. Perhaps she could get him down somehow. Unlikely if the fairy had used her supernatural powers to hold him in place. But she could climb up with him. Hold fast to him so that if the fairy hurled him down, she'd have to hurl Ceana, too. A small voice deep inside told her that the fairy wouldn't actually kill Gavran if it meant killing her too. No matter how much she threatened Ceana's death, it would go counter to what the fairy claimed to believe in so strongly. If she killed Ceana alongside Gavran, then Ceana would have, once again, sacrificed herself for a man.

The fairy lifted her chin, her gaze locked on Ceana. She seemed to be waiting for Ceana to agree with her.

Ceana stopped moving and shook her head. "Men like my dadaidh do exist." Memories of her time under the cursed side of the wishes tried to flood her mind. Her mouth went dry. She focused on trying to hear Gavran breathing a short distance from her instead. She couldn't catch the sound of it, but the act drove the thoughts away. "Evil, selfish men do exist. As do evil, selfish women. As do men who are trying to live in a way that pleases the Almighty. Like Gavran. Like Gavran's dadaidh Allen. Like Lord MacDonald and Eachann and—"

"Enough." The fairy's voice was sharp and sudden as a crack of thunder from a lightning strike far too close.

The fairy's expression was crumpled around the edges. Was it possible Ceana was getting through to her?

She couldn't take the chance. She moved another step closer to Gavran's position. Almost there. She'd have to tuck the fairy flag down the neck of her leine or toss it aside before she wrapped her arms around him. The risk of it touching his skin was too great otherwise.

Her throat spasmed, and she looked down at her palms. She clutched the fairy flag in one hand. Against her bare skin.

Maeve must have been mistaken. Touching the fairy flag clearly didn't make people without MacLeod blood go insane or she'd have already lost her wits and not been able to agree with the fairy this long.

In that case, the flag wouldn't hurt Gavran if it touched him.

She lunged for where Gavran balanced and grabbed for the edge of the embrasure to use as a stairstep to reach the top of the merlon.

She toppled backward as if unseen and unfelt hands had tugged her away. Her tailbone connected with the stones, and she bit back a cry.

"If you want to change the terms of our agreement to allow

cheating," the fairy's voice was honey again, "I'd be happy to make that amendment."

Fire licked inside Ceana. What she wanted to do was strangle the fairy with the tiny piece of cloth in her hands. She crawled to her feet. "You already cheated. I answered your question correctly, but you haven't given us your name and released us."

The fairy made a tisking noise. "You haven't answered my question correctly. You've only made general statements."

Maybe the stress of this situation had muddled her mind enough that she was no match for the fairy after all. "I don't understand."

The fairy made the flipping motion with her hand again. Gavran moved back so his heels hung over the edge. If the fairy released her hold on him, he'd have no hope of righting his balance or of Ceana reaching him in time. "The question you were to answer is why I bestowed *your* gift. You have one guess left."

CHAPTER 25

*C*eana's legs gave out, and she lowered herself to all fours on the tower stones. Grit embedded itself in her palms. Even after all the warnings she'd given herself, she still hadn't heard the nuances well enough.

Not why the fairy hated men. Not why the fairy sought to help women.

Why the fairy had picked her.

Ceana had thought of little else other than *why* in the over a year it'd been since the fairy first pulled them from the water. She was no closer to an answer now than she had been. Maybe with time. Maybe with the seelie council's advice. But she had neither.

And she had one guess left to figure it out.

A gust of wind lifted the fairy flag. Ceana grabbed it before the breeze could carry it over the edge. If by some miracle she figured out the answer, she'd have to be able to return it to the fairy or their bargain would be void.

She rolled into a sitting position. She didn't dare look at Gavran. She'd failed him.

She ran her finger over the delicate stitching of the fairy flag and peeked at the fairy. A compassion that could only come from the Almighty built inside her. The fairy hadn't always been this way. Once she'd been a wife who loved her husband. Once she'd been a mother who loved her child. She'd let bitterness rob her of that love.

A prickle ran over the back of Ceana's neck. Or had she?

She ran the fabric of the fairy flag through her fingers again. How had the story arisen that the fairy flag drove those without MacLeod blood mad if there wasn't a bit of truth in it?

Perhaps the MacLeods had spread the tale to keep people from trying to take the flag or a piece of it. But even that suggested they thought it had some power. Power left by a mother whose love ran so deep that she wanted to aid not only her child, but her child's child, and her child's child's child.

Ceana tried to swallow but her throat wouldn't work. The fairy hadn't only tried to help her. She'd tried to warn her mamaidh as well. Not random women. Women in the same family.

And she had held the fairy flag without going off her head from it.

Salome had said that humans who carried a touch of fae blood were more sensitive to the supernatural. It could explain why Ceana had been able to hear the banshee when Gavran couldn't. Why she'd seen through the keplie's disguise when Gavran saw only a horse.

Somewhere, long in her family's past, she'd descended from the fairy's son. Illegitimately most likely, which would have only made the fairy more compassionate towards her family line.

She got to her feet. The way to test her theory would be to touch the flag to Gavran's skin, but there was no way the fairy would allow that. And then they'd be back to the problem of how she'd manage to transport a mad Gavran back to Salome, Eliezer, and the seelie court.

She glanced up at Gavran. He watched her intently, his gaze

soft as if trying to tell her that he loved her no matter what happened.

A lump built in her throat, and her eyes burned. She had all the evidence she needed. Why did she keep looking for one more piece? She had to be the fairy's descendant. This must have all been about love. Misguided love, to be true, but still love.

Why then was it so hard for her to believe the words and speak them?

She clutched the fairy flag to her chest. Believing was hard because it meant she'd have to accept she was valuable enough for someone to go through all this for. Valuable enough without earning it in any way.

It was what Gavran had been trying to tell her, but she hadn't been able to hear him.

It was what the Lord God Almighty had been trying to tell her throughout all of Scripture, but she hadn't been ready to listen. She was flawed, aye. She sinned and hurt people and made bad choices. But God loved her anyway because He'd created her. Jesus loved her enough to die in her place, taking the punishment she deserved. She was loved and forgiven and made whole because she trusted in Him.

She had always been loved. She hadn't needed to earn it from her dadaidh. Or wait for it from Gavran. Her value came from God, not from any created being.

Others could love her even with all her flaws.

Now she had only to speak the words.

"You did it because you're my granaidh, many times back." She stepped forward and wrapped her arms around the fairy. "You did it because you love me."

Gavran came down like a puppet with its strings let loose, but instead of falling backward, he slid forward down the merlon in slow motion and landed on the ground.

And the fairy burst into tears.

CHAPTER 26

*I*mma.

The fairy's name was Imma. Even days later, standing in the cavern waiting for Eliezer to return from the seelie court, the thought brought rueful laughter to Ceana's throat.

"What's brought a smile to your face?"

Gavran spoke the words against her ear, and a shiver of warmth shot down into her belly. Salome's priest had wed them the night they'd returned to Duntulm Castle, and being married had only seemed to increase Gavran's desire to touch her.

He smiled against her ear. "Other than the obvious."

She turned slightly and placed a kiss to his jaw. "The fairy's name was a family name after all. My true granaidh's name was Imma."

"Would you have guessed it?"

She shook her head. Her granaidh might have been called Imma, but she had no idea how many other women in her family line might have taken their name from their fairy ancestor. Without the context she had now, she never would have thought to look to her own history for a guess.

The air shimmered, and Eliezer's large form filled the space in the cavern before them. His smile was brighter than the lanterns Salome had them bring to light the space while they waited.

"They've given me the authority to lift the wishes."

Gavran stood and pulled Ceana up with him. "Why didn't they do it themselves?"

Tension ran under Ceana's shoulder blades. Surely they weren't waiting to ask anything else of them. Something in Imma had crumbled—Ceana liked to think it was her resentment and unforgiveness—when Ceana called her granaidh and then wrapped her arms around her. She'd brought them back to Duntulm Castle herself, and she'd turned herself in to the seelie court for punishment.

Eliezer raised a hand as if he'd seen Ceana's fear and wanted to brush it away. "Imma asked that you be given a choice as recompense for the harm she caused you."

A choice? What kind of choice could there possibly be? She certainly wouldn't choose to remain under the cursed wishes. She grabbed Gavran's hand and linked her fingers tightly with his.

He gave her hand a gentle squeeze.

Eliezer lowered himself onto his giant boulder with a grunt. "You can be placed back to the moment where she saved you from drowning. You'll wake up sharing a nightmare of the fairy cursing you, not remembering how you got to land. It's what should have happened had the seelie court been aware of the cursed wishes when they happened."

Ceana's heart rose in her chest, and she opened her mouth to accept. She clamped her lips back shut before the words could come out. There was something very important missing from that offer. "What about everything that's happened since?"

"Gone. You'll have no memory of it because it won't have happened."

Gavran sucked in a sharp breath beside her.

Her body felt numb. She turned into Gavran and hid her face in his shoulder. She wouldn't have to live with the memories of that year under the wishes before she'd made it back to Gavran again. And her mamaidh and Colin...

Gavran pressed one hand to the back of her head and wrapped the other around her waist. "Her mamaidh will be alive again? Her brother back in her family home?"

It was like he'd read her mind. But her thoughts wouldn't exactly have been difficult to guess.

"Yes." Eliezer's answer was simple, but it felt like there were deep crevices spiderwebbing the space beneath it.

Ceana pulled free of Gavran's hold. Stepped back one pace to give herself space.

She'd not have to live with the soul-crushing things that happened to her in that year under the cursed wishes, but she'd also forget everything that had happened with Gavran in the weeks since they'd been reunited. She'd be back to being promised to Robbie Forsyth rather than wed to Gavran.

And that wouldn't be all that would be lost.

Gavran was watching her steadily. She met his gaze. Grabbed his hands.

"My mamaidh would be back, but Finn would be gone. Colin would be at home, but your mamaidh would be crippled. And Salome and Ihon and all the people on their land. The nuckalevee." She couldn't breathe. She tried to bring in air, but it wouldn't go down. "I don't want... I don't want..."

Gavran tugged her in and pressed his lips to hers. Gentle. Soothing. Full of love.

He eased back. She could breathe again.

He leaned his forehead against hers. "You're sure?"

She was sure of what she wanted. But she wasn't alone anymore. The monsters they'd fought might be something Gavran would rather forget. "I am, but this isn't my decision to make. It's ours."

"I like who I am now, with you." Gavran's words were low but steady. "We've made mistakes, but there's a lot of good we've done along the way. Like freeing the MacDonalds' people from the nuckalevee, as you said. And the Almighty knew what the fairy did, even if the seelie court didn't. He allowed it. I don't think the Almighty would have allowed this to happen to us if it hadn't been better somehow than if we hadn't suffered the way we have. I don't want to go back."

Her eyes stung. She was a better person, her faith in God stronger, her love for others deeper. She knew that without doubt. She wouldn't be this person without everything she'd gone through.

She straightened her shoulders and faced Eliezer. "Is our other option to have the curse lifted while everything else stays the same?"

Eliezer nodded.

"That's the option we choose."

EPILOGUE

*C*eana clutched the parcel full of food closer to her chest and turned down the alley behind the smithy. Today would be the day. She could feel it. Yesterday she'd been so close to getting him to agree.

She rounded the corner of the building. Colin's back was to her as he hung the dripping wash on the line, humming tunelessly to himself. The blacksmith's wife had been so suspicious when Ceana had come around asking questions, especially since when the woman asked Colin, he said he didn't have a sister. And his sweet, round face was too guileless for it to be a lie. To him, she'd still never existed. Over the last few weeks, though, the woman had seemed to come around as Colin warmed up to Ceana, starting to believe that it was Colin's slower mind that had him forgetting he'd once had a sister who'd been looking for him ever since he ran away from their relatives.

"Good morrow, Colin." She kept her voice soft. He startled easily at loud noises. Something that hadn't been the case before. "Would you like to share my food?"

He spun around, his face-splitting grin in place. "Ceana!" He ran to her and threw his arms around her, whacking her accidentally in the back with the wet pair of trews he still held in his hand. He drew back suddenly. "Did I squish the bairn?"

Ceana laid a hand on her mound of a belly. Before they'd finally found Colin in this tiny village on the coast after months of going town to town in an ever-widening circle around Dunvegan, both Gavran and Eachann had started to insist that they return to Duntulm. Soon. Neither of them wanted her giving birth away from Lyall and Maeve, should they be needed. Though she secretly suspected that Eachann was equally as anxious to simply see Maeve again.

"The bairn's nice and safe. You didn't squish him." She not-so-secretly wished her baby would be a boy, so he could grow up alongside Salome and Ihon's son the way Ihon and Eachann had grown up together. But Gavran was certain their baby was a girl.

Ceana opened her parcel of food. Sweet cakes with raisins, crisp apples, and fresh bread with cheese. All Colin's favorites.

He clapped his hands, then spun back to the wash line. "I have to finish my work first."

She helped him and then sat down on a stump while Colin flopped on the grass to eat. If she sat on the ground, she'd never get up without help.

He gobbled down the food as if he hadn't eaten in days, even though the blacksmith's wife assured her they fed him two meals along with their family in exchange for the little tasks he did for them. They still didn't know where he slept.

Colin gulped down the last bite of food and gave his stomach a happy pat.

Ceana folded up the cloth she'd used to bundle the food. "The bairn's going to come soon, and I have to go home before that happens." She, Gavran, and Eachann had talked it over for hours last night, and this approach had been Gavran's idea. He thought maybe Colin didn't understand what Ceana meant when she asked him to live with her. He might not understand she didn't live in the village where the blacksmith's family lived. "My home is a long way from here. I won't be able to see you anymore after I go home."

Colin's expression drooped. "Never?"

She and Gavran had no other reason to come back to MacLeod land other than Colin. While she'd been here, earning his trust, watched over by Eachann, Gavran had gone back to his family. It'd taken him almost as long to convince them of all that had happened, but they'd finally decided to pack up and move with Ceana and Gavran to MacDonald land. Gavran had only returned to her a couple of nights ago with the good news.

She wouldn't lie to Colin, but she also had to help him see why it was important he come with her. "Not for a long time at least because of the bairn."

Colin nodded solemnly, but tears built in his eyes.

Ceana took his hand. "I'd like you to come with me and be part of my family."

Colin rubbed his forefinger over his lips, up and down. "Would those men be there?"

Those men was what he called Gavran and Eachann. The blacksmith's wife had told her that Colin had a hard time trusting men. He still backed away if the blacksmith came too close. Growing up without Ceana to protect him from their dadaidh, Colin likely had plenty of reason. And they might never know what he'd gone through since he'd run away.

"Aye, they'll be there. Gavran..." She'd almost reminded Colin that Gavran was her bairn's dadaidh, but the last time she'd said that, he'd panicked and told her that she couldn't let that happen. Dadaidhs hurt children and mamaidhs. She'd cried so hard that night after she left him that she couldn't breathe. "Gavran loves and protects me. And Eachann is our friend. There'll be other people there too, but all of them are good and nice like the family you've been helping here."

Colin sucked his lips in and out. If he didn't agree, she could maybe convince Gavran to wait a couple more days. She couldn't leave Colin behind without feeling like she'd left a part of herself.

Finally, his head moved up and then down once. "I'll help him then."

Her throat closed, and she couldn't get words out.

"I'll help Gavran." Colin repeated as if he thought she hadn't spoken because she didn't understand what he meant. "I'm a good helper. I'll help him take care of you and the bairn."

She forced the lump in her throat to give way. "I know he'll like that. With you helping us, our family will be complete."

FREE BOOK OFFER

In 1500s Scotland, Ceana Campbell accidentally does the one thing every sensible Scottish woman knows better than to do. She angers a fairy. Now her only way out of a no-win situation seems to be to outwit a creature with supernatural intelligence.

Sign up for the author's mailing list and get a free copy of *Three Wishes*, the prequel to *Cursed Wishes*.

Visit www.subscribepage.com/threewishesstory to get started!

ABOUT THE AUTHOR

Marcy Kennedy is a fantasy author who believes there's always hope. Sometimes you just have to dig a little harder to find it. In a world that can be dark and brutal and unfair, hope is one of our most powerful weapons.

She also writes award-winning mysteries under a pen name, but that's a secret. Shhhh...

Marcy lives in Ontario, Canada, with her former Marine husband, eight cats (all rescues), a coonhound mix, and a budgie. In her free time, she loves playing board games and going for bike rides.

She also loves hearing from readers.

www.marcykennedy.com
marcy@marcykennedy.com